MILA
HILDEBRAND
IS
FOREVER NOT
YOURS

THE IMMORTAL MISTAKES BOOK THREE

SANDRA L. VASHER

MORTAL
INK PRESS

MORTAL
INK PRESS

To all the girls who have ever been counted out.
Count yourself in.

1.

MILA

2025 CE Earth

I am dying a slow, painful, exhausting, miserable death when it happens for what I think will be the last time.

Someone counts me out.

I'm lying on a flimsy cot in a crowded school gymnasium. They turned this place into a triage center after the attack. Biochemical terrorism. Someone set off a series of explosives in Los Angeles, releasing a deadly and highly contagious version of the influenza virus.

Now L.A. is a quarantine zone, there's a memorial with a six-block radius for all the victims who died in the actual blasts, and the perimeter wall is reserved for the thousands and thousands of us in make-shift hospitals all over the city. Our names are added to the wall on tiny gold plaques as we die.

Three months ago, I was a senior honors student in this high school, I'd just gotten the new coronavirus super vaccine, and my biggest problems were social phobia and mean girls on social media. Today, I'm coughing up my own blood and wondering if they'll spell my name right on my plaque. It's Mila Hildebrand. Not Mila Hildebrande. I watch as people die and the cots around me slowly empty out.

No one is allowed to visit, but there are plenty of tablets to go around. My parents video chat with me every day, and every day I watch them tear up when we say goodbye. They were on vacation in Napa Valley when it happened, while Freddie, Lara, and I were here. Lara, my older sister, was in the blast zone. Freddie, my younger brother, was with me at home. He died yesterday. Our parents had to watch on video, but I, at least, was holding his hand.

He was fourteen, and he was scared of dying.

I am scared of dying. I have lesions all over my skin, and it hurts to sit up, breathe, swallow. I can't get comfortable, so I roll onto my side, then flip to my other side. Six empty cots over, another teenager is sitting on the edge of his cot, hacking phlegm into a brown paper towel. I don't know him, so I don't think he went to this school. He is wispy thin and sallow pale like the dimmed yellow gym lights. He has long, elegant eyebrows and thick dark hair that only looks mildly mussed from days of fever sweat.

He catches me looking at him. His eyes are the color of dark roast coffee. The contrast between the darkness of his hair and eyes and the paleness of his skin makes him look like he stepped out of a Gothic anime. He's cute, and if I'd met him before, maybe I'd have tried to flirt with him. I don't really know how to flirt, though, and I think it might be rude now. We're on our deathbeds. Anything beyond eye contact is off the table.

He continues coughing but keeps his eyes on mine, and I have the feeling that he's thinking something similar about me. Though I don't know why. I cannot possibly look attractive lying in this filthy place.

A man and woman, both in business suits, come into the gym. They're not medical staff—the care workers always wear hazmat suits. They also aren't any of the government agents who sometimes show up armed only with a mask and gloves, but usually only to ask for a body count. Those agents always have a zombie look, like they can't believe there are *still* more people to add to the death toll.

The man and woman who just came into the gym don't have the *look*, and apparently, they don't think they're at risk of dying from exposure. Neither wears a mask. They go patient-by-patient, checking off what must be names on a list and only rarely stopping, but not seeming to care if they get too close.

When they reach the cot where the boy with the dark eyes is sitting, they stop. I'm feverish, and I hear everything in that muffled way that happens when your whole head is congested. So maybe I hear wrong, but what I think the woman says is, "Christian Godric. Eighteen. Musical savant."

I laugh softly into my pillow. *Godric* might be a worst last name than my own, *Hildebrand*. Those are the kind of last names you get bullied for.

I hear the man say, "take him," and the woman jots something down on the list. They move on to another patient, then stop by me. I become worried that my fever is worse than I realized. These two have bright red eyes. Like they're wearing red-colored contact lenses.

"Mila Hildebrand," the woman says. "Honor roll."

The man gazes at me, and I feel like he is stripping me down, not to the skin but to something else. Something worse. Something intangible.

It takes less than five seconds.

"Move on," he says coldly.

They go on to the next patient, and the boy—Christian—shrugs at me. I guess neither of us knows what that was about, and I don't feel good enough to care. It is interesting that Christian is some kind of musical genius, though. I wonder what he plays. A string instrument, I decide. He doesn't look hardy enough for brass, and he doesn't seem delicate enough for woodwind. Maybe he plays the cello.

I don't play anything. My genius is physics genius. Astrophysics. I'm in love with the stars. But I wanted to be an astronaut, not the Little Prince. Christian lies on his side facing me, and we watch each other until I fall into a restless sleep. When I wake, it's to some commotion. He is being moved onto a stretcher and carried out. I can't tell if he's still alive.

A nurse is taking my vitals. She puts a clip on my finger.

"What's happening?" I ask groggily.

The nurse frowns and removes the instrument. "I'm going to give you more M3."

That's bad. M3 is a new, morphine-like pain med, laced with an anti-anxiety drug. It's commonly used at the euthanasia clinics that started popping up around the country in the wake of the pandemics of the early 2020s. They don't give it to you because you're getting better.

"Where did they take him?" I say.

"Don't worry about that," the nurse says.

"Did he die?"

She sighs, and I think she's young, but her eyes are dull and tired. "No. He's a candidate for some kind of experimental treatment. He might recover."

Recover. I had erased that word from my mind, but now it sounds like a magical oasis of life.

"I want to try," I croak out. "Can I … volunteer?"

She squeezes my hand. "They're not selecting based on how sick you are. That boy is a violinist with the L.A. Philharmonic. They say he's one of the best in the world."

That hits me hard. So what, I wasn't *special* enough? They're only choosing savants, and my talents didn't *count*? I have an IQ of *170*.

"Guess smart wasn't good enough," I whisper.

The nurse hums. "Oh, sweetheart. It's okay. Hardly anyone is *that* special. But you're a natural beauty, alright. I bet you were a cheerleader *and* on the student council. Were you homecoming queen? You probably had all the boys."

Homecoming queen? Student council? *Cheerleader?* What is she talking about? I was a science fair champ and the president of the AI club. I've been to space camp three times. I was taking graduate-level physics classes because I did all the high school classes in middle school. I have, like, ten comic book-related t-shirts.

"I'm too smart for boys," I tell her ruefully.

She laughs. "Well, good for *you*. Maybe if you're lucky, that spunk will pull you out of this."

They shouldn't say stuff like that when we all know no one pulls out of this kind of illness with just spunk. No. There was no way out before, and those two people in the suits came here to pluck patients who mattered out of the masses, but they didn't pick *me*.

I don't understand. Did they look into my history at all? If they had, wouldn't they have found *something* worth saving? But I can think of an explanation for why they didn't bother. It's an ugly truth that has never served me well. People always said I looked exactly like my sister, Lara, who was a blond-haired, brown-eyed bombshell beach babe.

I've never had the confidence to flaunt it like Lara did, or the interest, and no normal guy wants to date a girl who babbles about quantum mechanics when she gets nervous. But that doesn't mean I haven't noticed that men frequently fail to look me in the eye. I suppose when you're dying on a hospital cot, and your throat is too swollen to talk about much of anything, all anyone has to judge you by is your looks. And I look like a dumb little girl. They probably think I slept my way onto the honor roll.

The nurse watches me swallow two M3 tablets. "I was going to be a space astronaut," I croak out to her before she leaves me. I do not know why I say it or why I say it so ineloquently. Fever, probably. I fall back into a restless sleep and dream about seeing Christian Godric again.

Several weeks follow, during which I barely know what is real. I expect to die in that gym. I think the nurses are gossiping about me. Someone comes to take my body away, and when they lift me onto the stretcher, I assume I am dead. But the morgue is a cold laboratory where they start an IV in my arm, put oxygen tubes in my nose, hook me up to a million machines, and make me feel even worse than I felt before. I beg for more M3. My parents show up not wearing masks or hazmat suits or anything. I see Christian in the doorway a few times, but his eyes are bright red, so that can't be right.

As it turns out, however, I'm not dying. I'm healing without even knowing it. And one day, I wake up feeling like all the pain has left my body. I'm tired, but I'm also hungry. My head doesn't ache anymore. My throat isn't swollen. I can breathe without hurting my lungs.

A doctor comes into the room, and she has those same red eyes. "Ahh, Mila! You're awake," she says. "Good for you! We didn't think you were going to make it. That nurse really threw a fit to get you in here."

I surprise myself with the strength to sit up. "What happened?"

"We admitted you to a very special program," the doctor says. "It's called the Immortality Program. Have you heard of it?"

I nod. Yes. I've read all about it, but it seemed too far-fetched to ever affect me. The Immortality Program is a brand new thing where they give people who are about to die an injection of a highly-engineered drug they call the Immortality Virus.

The virus isn't that different from the one used in the terrorist attacks, except it's survivable. Hits you like the flu, wreaks havoc on your system, but as your body fights off the virus, your physiology and cellular chemistry change, and your immune system becomes super-charged. When you recover—*if* you recover—you will only ever age to an optimal level of physical health, usually somewhere in your late twenties. After that, you can still be killed by accident, but illness hardly touches you and you remain perpetually young.

"So am I ... immortal?" I ask the doctor.

She holds up a hand mirror. "Would you like to see the evidence? Unfortunately, this is a side effect we can't control. But it's a minor thing, and you can get color contact lenses later if you want."

I take the hand mirror and hold it up so I can see my face. I look thin and a little tired, and my eyes are bright red.

I'm immortal.

2.

CHRISTIAN

I do not like people. At best, most humans are hypocritical and petty. At worst, they are stupid and mean. Humans lie and cheat and steal. They make up their own moral codes and break them. Given a choice between a selfless decision and a selfish decision, they nearly always choose what will be most destructive to everyone but themself.

So, given a choice between the company of a human and the company of my violin, I always choose the violin. The violin will do exactly what I ask, sing back to me, communicate wonderful things to me. If it breaks my heart, it will be because it is too beautiful, not because it cannot be trusted.

I do not like people.

But Mila Hildebrand is an exception from the start, and it isn't because *she* is beautiful, though she *is* that. As far as I can see, she is the most beautiful human ever made. Even lying on her deathbed in a sea of sickness, barely able to lift her head, emaciated from weeks of physical deterioration, covered in lesions, all I see when I look at her is the pinnacle of creative evolution.

Her facial features, gaunt as they are now, are sharply feminine. The curve of her figure under that horrible cotton bedding is the curve of a viola. Her lips are slightly parted and cracked when she pants for air, and yet, when she sees me staring at her, they form into a perfect, blood-stained pout. It's her own blood. We're all coughing up blood.

But most importantly, her eyes—polished mahogany, with ripples of clover honey—crackle with a recognition that tells me this girl doesn't miss a thing. She's smart and powerful, and I see in her eyes a woman who never suffers from human flightiness. One day, she will command her environment. She will be the one they all bend around. She will be a *goddess*.

The moment I make that connection, I am changed. Before her, there wasn't anyone I truly wanted. I scarcely understood physical attraction at all. I'd traveled the world playing in concert venues from L.A. to Dubai, and no girl ever sparked more than surface-level lust in me. But this one? I'd have dropped Stradivari's La Pucelle to touch her just once.

When they carry me away from that stench hole gymnasium, I am too delirious to know what is happening except that I am being taken from her. When I wake up in an unfamiliar medical facility, and they tell me I am now immortal, the first thing I feel is an overwhelming loss. Loss of her. But when I later find out that she, too, has been brought to this strange complex to be transformed into an immortal, I feel the universe has confirmed all my suspicions.

She is a goddess.

I was *made* to worship her.

And her eyes are only more gorgeous red.

I have a preference for observing before I act, so I don't strike up a conversation with her at the first chance I get. It is a wise move, because Mila behaves somewhat differently than I expected. I watch her come into the medical facility's small dining hall with her thin shoulders hunched in around her like armor the first day she is able. She sits alone. She reads a book while she eats. She avoids eye contact so much that her eyes never meet mine. I don't think she even knows I'm there. When she is finished eating, she leaves immediately.

This is not how a goddess should be. Unnoticed. Unseen. If I don't want company at dinner, I achieve that by looking up and snarling at anyone who tries to sit by me. I do not understand why Mila tries to make herself invisible rather than snarling herself.

The medical facility is just one building of a larger complex called the Los Angeles Immortality Center. The room I am recovering in has a nice view of a well-maintained garden, and I happen to see my goddess venture outside there the next afternoon. She shuffles out in a hospital robe, sits down on a wooden bench, and pulls out that book again. It must be hotter than it looks because she pushes the robe off her shoulders after a while, allowing the sun to drench the bare skin of her neck while she reads.

This is how I imagine serenity looks. But then three teenage boys enter the garden, and when they see her, one of them whistles and the other two chortle after the first. Mila pulls the robe up, puts her head down, and slips back inside like she was never anything but a shadow out there when really, she was the light.

I have never thought of myself as violent, but those punks stay in the garden after Mila leaves, goofing around and making lewd gestures, and it makes me want to gouge out their eyes.

I'm not ready yet for a formal introduction, but I can't let that just go. I decide to take a little stroll inside, making a point to pass her room, pause in the doorway, and watch her until she notices me standing there. Her face relaxes, and she smiles at me. I smile back. She says, "hi." I say, "hi." Then I leave and return to my own room.

The dining hall is more crowded the next evening, and I can't find an empty table. I choose to take a place that will give me a view of the door, and that puts me between two other guys who seem to be my age.

They introduce themselves before I can snarl at them.

"I'm Phelps," the one to my right says. He is beefy, and he has red curly hair and acne-scarred skin.

"Zaden," the other says. He is skinny, and he has a shaved head and a tattoo on his neck. I understand why there was an empty seat between the two of them.

I consider ignoring them both, but I'm in a new community, and it is sometimes useful to have allies. Especially when you are trying to acquire information about a third party.

"Christian Godric," I say.

"No shit," Zaden says. "Violinist Christian Godric?"

"You listen to classical music?" I ask, feeling genuinely surprised. My name is known in the right circles, but Zaden doesn't seem like the type who would be in those circles.

Still, I now realize that his tattoo is the logo for a wildly popular crunk pop band I am only vaguely familiar with. I can't actually remember the name of the band, but the Immortality Program is selective. I suppose it would make sense for rock stars to qualify.

He grins like he knows I just put it together. "Zaden Omega." He sticks his hand out toward me. "Lead singer of 'Z Howl."

"Ahh." I have a steak and a salad on my plate. I carve into the steak rather than shake the guy's hand. I need allies, not friends. "You named your band after yourself."

Zaden smirks. "What else do you name your band after? I can't believe I'm sitting next to Christian Godric. I love rock violin."

"I do not play *rock* violin," I say.

"But there are some awesome rock remixes of what you do play on BeatSpot," Zaden says.

"What is rock violin?" Phelps asks.

Luckily, I can largely ignore that question while Zaden, who is apparently a fan of mine, launches into an explanation of how good classical music is sometimes bastardized for unholy purposes.

In the meanwhile, Mila walks in. She takes a look around, sighs, picks up a tray, and goes through the food line as quickly as possible. Once she has her dinner, she looks around again. There are plenty of tables with seats but not a single empty table. She walks toward a table where two girls are chatting. The girls begin laughing just as Mila starts walking their way.

I don't think they're laughing at her, but Mila seems to think it is rejection. She takes a visible breath and aims her tray at another table where a mixed-gender group of older teens is talking. As soon as those kids notice her coming their way, they spread their trays out toward the fourth seat so that it will be harder for her to sit there. Probably not personal, but it still sucks.

She cringes and then spots a single table where one of the nurses is sitting alone. Mila sits down with the woman, who is doing something on her phone and doesn't bother looking at Mila. Mila eats her dinner in less than ten minutes. She is gone before Phelps has decided that the 'Z Howls should include strings in their next big hit, and I have decided that Phelps is here because he is rich.

A rock star and a rich kid. Those are not bad allies.

Since it is easier not to look like a stalker if I'm not alone, I suggest to Zaden and Phelps that we take a walk together around the facility after dinner. Mila has gone back to her room, and she is sitting on her bed with her knees pulled up to her chin, staring out the window.

I tell my two lackeys that I'm tired after we pass her room, and I return to my room. None of this is right. What is a girl like Mila doing disappearing into a hospital bed? I stay up late, staring out my own window at that garden, and I catch a lucky break at midnight when I see Mila come into the garden again. This time, she takes the robe off entirely, tosses it over the bench like an act of rebellion, and soaks up the moonlight in pajama pants and a camisole while she reads.

Now is the time for the formal introduction.

I grab my own robe, shove on my shoes, and I'm down there in the garden with her a few minutes later. Initially, I'm not sure if she knows I'm there, but as I approach, she puts her book down and says, "Are you following me, Christian Godric?"

The goddess remembers my name.

"I have you under observation, Mila Hildebrand," I answer, and it takes everything in me not to make that sound breathless.

She's had a bad day. She does not smile at the fact that

I know her name, and I don't know exactly what else to say to her. That's what being moonstruck by a goddess will do to you. You can be the smartest person in the universe and forget how to speak in a moment like that.

She looks up at the stars. "I don't know if I like it here," she says. "It seems like things should be different now that we're immortal, but people are still the same to me. They jeer at me. They shut me out. I don't know what I do to make them act like that." She points up at the moon. "I wish I could just live up there, alone, you know? Maybe with an internet connection."

I've had thoughts like that before, and I think I'm falling for her, and I don't know it then, but that moment is sealing both my destiny and hers.

"I wouldn't even need the internet," I tell her. "Just a violin. I would play for the stars."

"I bet the stars listen better than any human ever could," she says. She is still gazing at the moon, but I am not. I'm looking at her and thinking what I just said was a lie. I would need my violin, and I would need her.

She shifts her gaze away from the sky and catches me staring at her, and it is the first time I ever remember blushing over something like that.

"I thought you played the cello," she says.

She keeps surprising me. It makes me laugh. "I don't like people enough to be a cellist."

She folds her hands in her lap. "I like people. But I don't trust them. I trust physics and math equations and books. They do what I ask them to do. It's why I never have any friends, I guess."

I wonder what it is that makes it so that she knows she can say things like that to me? She can. I'm exactly the person she can say things like that to. I want to tell her that, but timing is everything, and it feels like it's still her turn.

"I like you, Christian," she says. "And for some reason, I trust you. But if you're trying to be my friend, you should probably move on. I'm not good with people."

That's my moment. "Friendship is not what I had in mind," I tell her.

"Hmm," she says.

I take one step toward her. Two. Three. Then I reach out with both hands, touch her shoulders. I am observant, I am smart, and I do not like most people.

"The ones who jeer at you do it because they are stupid and mean, and they don't care if their eyes are a violation of your personal space," I tell her, disregarding entirely the way the pads of my thumbs are lightly brushing her skin. That's not a violation. There's nothing in her facial expression warning me to stop. "The others are hypocritical and petty, so they are both afraid and jealous of you, and they handle it by doing petty things to avoid you and make you feel small."

I push her shoulders back lightly until she is sitting up straight and looking wide-eyed and curious at me. I believe her eyes were *always* meant to be red.

"And you can't stop them, so you might as well be looking up when it happens. Otherwise, how will you use the power you have to make them react?"

It has become cold enough outside that I can see the hint of her breath in the air. She puts her hands over mine, and I feel an electricity that makes me warm before she removes my hands from her shoulders.

"I would like for you to play for me sometime," she says softly.

"I can make that happen," I say.

3.

MILA

2035 CE Earth

One thing I expected, in the beginning, is that immortality would make me feel like I had all the time in the universe to do anything I wanted. But here's a secret mortals don't know: having a longer life span doesn't make your life seem longer. It only makes your days go faster.

I blink my red eyes, and I've been living at the L.A. Immortality Center for a decade. I have a Ph.D. in astrophysics, I have a job with ImmortalSpace, and I am researching potential destination planets for a massive program scheduled to launch Earth's first real interplanetary colonization program fifty years from now. I still want to be an astronaut, but I don't know if I'll ever be one. There are … obstacles.

Christian says I need to blow past those obstacles, but things are never as easy for me as he seems to think they should be. I worry about this, and I think it affects our relationship. I'm not sure why. He is my only confidant. Whenever he is home in L.A., he spends all his time with me. As far as I know, he has never dated anyone else.

And yet, he is not my boyfriend. His lips have never touched mine. We have never cuddled. I can't imagine the words, "I love you," coming out of his mouth. I'm glad he's never said it. He seems to hold this idealized version of me in his mind like a light that never goes out, and I don't live up to it in reality. If he told me he loved me, I'd always think he was talking about that idealized me.

If he loves me, I want it to be true.

One evening, he is in my apartment. There are empty cartons of Chinese food littering my kitchen table. I have my legs stretched out over the sofa, and I am studying brand new images obtained with the Elon Interstellar Telescope. They're of a potential destination planet I'm particularly intrigued by.

This is a huge accomplishment, and it's all mine. I was the one who came up with the plans for the Elon Interstellar Telescope when I was a grad student. I was the one who secured private funding from ImmortalSpace with an out-of-this-world grant application. I led the team that developed the telescope, and now I am the lead researcher on the team that uses the telescope.

The planet I'm looking at is one of fifteen that I've hand-picked based on our research as a potential planet for human colonization. One day, immortal humans will *live* on this planet. If I manage to become an astronaut, maybe *I'll* live there.

The thought awes me. I look up from the photos and see Christian standing near a window. He is tuning his violin while the light of a sunset seeps through the gauzy curtains he helped me hang when I first moved in. I stop thinking about my planet for just a moment while I watch him get lost in the sound of the strings he is tuning. I think he hears something in them that normal people just can't. Something out-of-this-world.

He doesn't take too long to finish tuning his violin, and when he is done, he starts playing something I haven't heard before. It starts slow and haunting, begins building—he catches me watching him during that part, his lips curl up, and then he turns his back to me and faces the red sunlight—and for a few minutes, I watch his shoulders rise and fall with the intensity of the music he commands.

When he's done, he stands still, letting the final note linger, and when he turns back around, I'm thinking of what he would be like as a lover. He meets my eyes and wets his lips, and I assume that means he likes my skin flushed. He's not my boyfriend, but it's not because there is no physical attraction between us.

He sets down his violin, comes over to the sofa, and sits on the armrest casually as if nothing especially interesting is happening between us right now.

"Tell me about the new planet," he says.

This is how it always goes. Any moment that might turn into something more always gets cut short by one of us.

I force my mind away from his passions and onto my own. "It's a perfect Goldilocks," I tell him. "Similar natural landscapes to Earth. Oceans. Mountains. Valleys. Rivers. Ice caps and snow near the poles. Tropical islands near the equator. And as the telescope gets closer, it's sending us more and more detailed pictures. I think the place has carbon-based life. Its foliage would feel familiar. It has its own animals and birds. I even have a picture of these furry critters that look kind of like a cross between a cat and a rat."

"So, a muskrat?" Christian says.

"A cat with a skinny tail and a pointy nose."

I swipe over to a picture of the animal and sit up to show him. He sits down next to me on the sofa and patiently lets me flip through dozens and dozens of photos.

"See, look," I say, pointing to a picture of the whole planet. "There are two main continents, but one is much bigger than the other."

"So where would we live?" he asks, and I think it's cute that he literally means us. Me and him. Because he assumes that my astronaut dreams will come true and that he will, of course, come with me wherever I want to go.

I show him the smaller of the main continents and point to an island off the continent's west coast. "This is where I would build the first human settlement." I zoom in closer and give him a virtual tour of the island. "There don't seem to be any natural predators that a human with a hunting rifle couldn't take down. There's an abundance of trees with what looks like some kind of fruit. We could probably genetically modify those to make them edible if they aren't already. But it's lush, so if not, we could grow Earth plants there. There's this gorgeous white beach ..."

"Looks like Hawaii," Christian says.

"I've never been," I tell him.

He laughs. "We better fix that before we leave for this planet. Or you won't know what to compare it to. Is there any intelligent life on the planet?"

"Maybe." I switch to some pictures of the larger continent and point out some of the places where instead of land or water, all we can see are bubbles of nothing. "These are mostly only on this side of the planet, and my colleagues think they're shadows from one of the planet's two moons or clouds or something." I move one of the photos around. "But look at that. They're always located exactly where a valley or clearing would be, given the surrounding topography."

"Not random enough for clouds," Christian says.

"Exactly. I think those are settlements or cities of some kind, and the native intelligent life form is smart enough to be blocking out our cameras."

He takes the tablet from me and looks closely at the pictures. "But they don't have satellites, do they? How intelligent can they be?"

"Hard to say when we can't see them."

"So, we have no idea how threatening they might be."

Now I laugh. "*Humans* are extremely threatening. If we ever make it to this planet, we'll probably be the dangerous species." I notice his violin lying on my coffee table. "Do you suppose they listen to music?"

He gives my tablet a dirty look. "If they don't, we shall crush them into the ground and take their planet from them. Any life form that cannot appreciate music is not worthy of the land they walk on."

"What if they don't walk or hear?"

His expression goes especially dark. "Then we'll shoot them out of the sky. No music, no respect." It's a little scary, but as soon as he sets the tablet down, his expression lightens again. "Not that I have that much respect for most of my fellow humans. When are we leaving?"

"You assume we're going on this trip together."

"We are," he says. "You're going, because someone has to lead the expedition. I'm going because you're going."

Now *my* expression darkens. There will be an application process for any space program, and I have been training to be an astronaut for years. I would pass all the tests, qualify on every level. If we do go to this particular planet, I'll know more about it than anyone else in the world. But these things are political, and despite my success with the Elon Interstellar Telescope, I don't exactly have friends at ImmortalSpace. I'm still not good at making friends. I can't imagine anyone wanting to be in space with me for thousands of years.

"Not likely," I tell Christian, and he does something he hardly ever does. He leans over, puts his hand behind my neck, and tilts my head toward his like he's going to kiss me. It amps up all the tension between us and all my anxiety with it. He has never kissed me before.

"Mila, you are *not* going without me. Don't you know that by now?"

I *never* think about life without Christian. It's simply implausible. I blink at him in surprise. "I didn't mean *that.*" My voice comes out soft, and I see his microsecond-glance at my lips. "It's just that *you* probably have a better chance than I do of getting on any ship going into space."

His eyebrows pinch together, and he inches closer to me. "That is *your* planet, Mila Hildebrand. You *will* be on the ship that goes there. You *will* be leading the expedition that lands on it. You have *no idea* how powerful you're going to be someday. You'll rule that planet."

He says things like this sometimes, but it always feels bittersweet to me. It's him idolizing me for reasons I don't understand.

"You're the only person who thinks that."

"I don't *think* it. I *know* it." His eyes get intense when he talks like this, and I can't look away from that deep red. "Things will be different by the time we get to that planet. *You* will be different. *We* will be different."

But that only makes me feel kind of miffed at him. I pull back and pout. "Christian, if the only reason you're spending time with me is you think I'm going to *change* drastically and become someone else—"

"That isn't what I'm saying." He lowers his voice, and it makes me feel the electricity that's always there between us buzz like a million pricks of static touching my skin. "You don't need to become someone else. You only need to change enough to feel your own strength. And it *will* be different between us when you stop feeling so vulnerable. When you realize you're in control."

He is not talking about me as an astronaut or a researcher anymore, and it gives me the sudden urge to test this theory he's putting forth. Why hasn't anything between Christian and me ever gone further than this? Is it me? If I had the same confidence in myself that he has, would that make me the person he believes I am? Is who I am merely a matter of perception?

"What are you going to call it?" he asks.

"Call what?" I say.

He raises a well-groomed eyebrow. "Your planet."

"Oh," I say while the intensity of that buzz I'm feeling increases my bravery. I lean toward him. "Kepler—" my lips are nearly touching his "—I want this to be *the* planet Kepler."

My lips make contact with his, and the match feels like something we were made for. All that electricity bounces around inside me like sparks looking to ignite a flame, and I don't know why I never tried this before. I should have. I should have done this *years* ago. Because now that we're doing this, all I can feel is him, and all I can think is how do I feel *more* of him?

I press my hands against his chest, and our mouths open. He puts his hand on my neck again, but his lips are quivering against mine, and when he curves his other hand around my waist, it seems so hesitant. Does he not want me kissing him? But no, he's kissing back with as much vigor as I'm giving him, if not more, and his hands feel good on me. So maybe he's just afraid to make any sudden movements because he knows that might ignite those sparks flickering between us. Then we'll be burning up in a fire we don't know how to put out.

I'm not prepared for that, either, so I hold on to that kiss until I absolutely have to stop, then I pull away. He makes this noise like a hiss of breath and loss mixed together, and he makes removing his hands from me feel like a caress, and it sends my mind whirling.

"See?" he whispers. "Everything is yours. You only have to decide when you're going to take it."

"What if I want you, Christian?" I whisper back.

His eyes are naturally a darker red than mine because his original eye color was a deeper brown. With his pupils dilated, it's like he has embers burning in his eyes, and when he draws in a breath at my words, I regret choosing to be cautious this time.

His eyes soften on the exhale, and it gives me that feeling I sometimes have that he can see directly into my mind. He picks up my hand and kisses the back of it while his lips curl into a tiny, knowing smile.

"You have time, Mila," he says. "I'm forever yours."

4.

MILA

2044 CE Earth

Another decade goes by, and my dream of traveling to Kepler starts to feel more like a goal than a fantasy. Before immortality was practical, getting to another planet would have required a ship that could go faster than anything humans could build. Now we only need a ship that's sturdy and sustainable enough to survive a journey of several thousand years.

ImmortalSpace starts building prototypes and taking applications from civilians who want to use their immortality to see the universe. ImmortalSpace targets fifteen planets for exploration based on my research, then it selects fifteen expedition teams.

I request a spot on the expedition team for my favorite planet, and I should be a shoo-in for the lead. After all, I know more about my planet than anyone else, and I now have expertise in astrophysics, astroengineering, molecular biology, chemical engineering, and intergalactic planetary exploration.

I get a spot, but not as the lead. Instead of selecting

someone with real expertise, ImmortalSpace chooses Jared Silvey as our team captain. It's political, and everyone knows it. Silvey is a privileged white man with a business background, an over-ripened sense of self, and zero knowledge about our planet. Why couldn't they have found a privileged white man with a military background instead? Silvey is completely underqualified.

His second-in-command, Renfield Bray, introduces Silvey in his absence at our first team meeting because Silvey's apparently too important to introduce himself or attend the meeting. He is busy golfing. Bray is Silvey's slightly younger, privileged white male mentee, and he looks at me like eye contact with the team secretary is overrated.

Yes. The team secretary.

Bray calls roll at our first meeting, and when he calls the name of our actual secretary, Eldyre Dresden, he looks around, zeroes in on my blouse like he has x-ray vision, and says, "Ms. Dresden. Pleasure to have you on the team. Your office has been set up between mine and the captain's."

I am not their secretary.

Also, Dresden deserves more respect, too. He is a man with an ivy-league education, degrees in group psychology, accounting, finance, and communication, and a very hot super-model boyfriend. I've known Dresden for at least ten years, and we aren't friends, but I've always liked him. I like him now as he gives me a little eye-roll before he lifts a hand and says, "uh, sir, I'm Eldyre Dresden."

"Oh, uh," Bray stutters over the mistake.

"I'm Mila Hildebrand," I say. "The team's lead planetary researcher?"

Bray looks over the list like maybe my name isn't on there, and when he finds it, he just says, "Uh-huh. Okay, well, looks like you know your way around here, Mila."

This isn't the first time I've dealt with this problem. Far from it. I get treated like a moron and/or piece of meat all the time, even at work. Middle-aged men flirt with me, young men check out my ass, old men make inappropriate comments about my looks.

Last year, I went to a conference on behalf of Immortal-Space to talk about our space program. I took an intern, and we were both immortal, so even though he was only twenty-four and I was thirty-five, we both looked like we were in our late twenties. Do you know what happens when a man and a woman in their late twenties show up to a conference together? I do. People still assume the man is the boss and the woman is his assistant.

In 2044.

I'm not even kidding.

That's probably why I hardly think twice about Lieutenant Sexist Renfield Bray after I meet the rest of the group. I'm far more concerned with two other astrophysicists on the team. Wren Augur and Delphine Vardelle. They're listed on the team roster as "assistant" planetary researchers. That should make me their boss, but they both seem to have something against me from the beginning.

At first, I think it's all in my head. Just because I sit alone and eat lunch in my office every day while the two of them go out together doesn't mean they're gossiping about me. Just because Wren is always correcting me in front of Silvey and Bray doesn't mean she's trying to sabotage me.

But there's, "Here's Mila's report—" she smiles at me "—don't worry, I corrected those three typos on page two before I made copies for everyone."

And then there's, "You mean antimatter, right? Not

anti-gravity? Were *you* the one who mixed those up right before that accident with the rocket that blew up last year?"

Still, Wren, at least, gives off an air of intelligence, and I would rather deal with her disdain than Delphine's passive aggression. Delphine is like a mean girl in a candy wrapper. She comes to the office every day dressed like she stepped out of a fashion blog. She wears perfect makeup. She flirts with Silvey and Bray.

And when we're alone, she makes these biting little comments meant to shake my confidence. "Mila, are dumpy turtlenecks in season?" "Gold eyeshadow *again*, Mila? If you're wearing it to make your eyes look less tired, it isn't working."

Christian says they're threatened by me and the solution is to show them that they can't beat me, but I don't see how I'm supposed to do that. Every interaction I have with them turns out badly for me.

Like the afternoon we name my planet.

"Where do you think we should land?" Delphine asks Wren as we are discussing the planet in a routine meeting that day. This is how things go with them. They talk to each other like I'm not even there. Like I don't have opinions worth knowing.

"Well, obviously, the island—" I start to say.

Wren points to the very center of the mainland continent, at a spot not too far from one of those places in the photos we have that show up as blurry bubbles instead of clear pictures of anything.

"Here," she says confidently. "It's near a freshwater lake and a huge set of waterfalls. We'll be able to harness electricity immediately."

I try to speak up. "Yeah, but there's the risk of—"

"Oh, I agree," Delphine says, cutting me off like I never

said anything. "And it's in a mild, temperate climate."

She's got that wrong. "Actually, that area is going to be relatively cold in—"

"Have you thought about what we should name it?" Wren says. To Delphine again. Not me. But I don't want *this* one messed up.

"Kepler," I say right away, loudly. "We should name it Kepler. After the astronomer and the first telescope that detected this planet."

"Other planets are already called Kepler," Wren says.

"Other planets are *coded* with the word Kepler," I say. "Kepler 22b and such. But this one deserves to be *the* planet Kepler."

Wren and Delphine share a look I associate with nefarious plotting, and we break soon after that. But the next afternoon, we have a meeting with Bray to present an initial landing plan. Wren starts with, "As you know, Planet X2187910—" and Bray immediately cuts her off.

"Are we *really* still calling it that?" he says.

Bray's an ass to Wren, which only mildly appeases me. At least if he's an ass to her, it means he respects her intelligence. He still doesn't know how to look me in the eye.

I see a flash of panic in Wren's face, though, and then she glances quickly at me. I am opening my mouth to suggest Kepler when she says:

"*I* was thinking we should call it Kepler. After the first telescope to find this planet. This place is magnificent, and it is probably the first humans will ever colonize. It deserves to be *the* planet Kepler."

"Kepler," Bray says. He scratches his chin like he's deep in thought. "I like it."

After that, the planet is called Kepler, and Wren takes

credit for it.

"Don't be bitter, Mila," Wren says to me much later. "You got your way, didn't you?"

I hate that woman.

Maybe things on the expedition team would have stayed that way—a stable level of simmering anger between me and everyone else—if The Incident never happened. Maybe things wouldn't have gotten worse at all if ImmortalSpace had stopped hosting those First Friday happy hours after a woman got sexually assaulted at one, back in 2032. But about a year after our team is chosen, Bray gets drunk at one of those happy hours, and I happen to be working late the same night.

He decides to leave work when I do. I get into an elevator with him. Just me and him. The doors close. I can smell alcohol on him all the way from the other side of the elevator. And maybe he takes my sideways glance as flirting or something because it seems like only a few seconds pass between when I notice that he is drunk and when he smashes me against the back wall and starts trying to hump me like a dog while he's sticking his nasty hand where it should not go.

I *do* try to fight back, but I'm too stunned to scream. The first thing I actually manage to get out of my mouth after the assault begins is "security camera." I say it while half-pointing at the camera with my hand, which he has restrained at the wrist.

He looks up toward where I'm pointing, and his stupid drunken face makes him look like a little boy who got caught with his hand in the cookie jar. Except I'm not his fucking cookie jar.

Bray gets fired. I get called into Silvey's office, and he says, "I'm sorry, Miss … Hilda?" He looks up, but his eyes don't quite make it to mine. "Always knew Bray was a pig. Should've fired him myself. But I've interviewed the rest of the team, and everyone just feels so bad about how this has affected your mentality. We're transferring you to mission control to make you more comfortable."

Mission control? Those people aren't going to *any* of the planets. They're grounded on Earth.

"But—" I say.

"What did you say you do?" Silvey says with a smarmy smile. Good news, he *can* make eye contact. Bad news, he follows that up with, "You're the admin, right? Well, our accounting and personnel reports have been top-notch. I'm sure they'll be happy to have a girl like you on the ground."

"But I'm not—" I try again.

"I'm sorry," he says, chuckling to himself. "I just have to tell you. You have beautiful eyes."

I get up feeling too stupified to do anything else, and I'm sure his eyes follow my ass out the door. Later, my boss in mission control—a hard-to-crack woman with more degrees than I have—is happy to treat me like a scientist, but I'm officially out. I'm not going to Kepler.

Christian finds out about what happened from one of the two guys who follow him around everywhere. I don't know how they know, but I suppose word of a scandal always travels fast, and the immortal community isn't that big yet.

I am nervous that Christian will be angry at me for not telling him immediately. He isn't. He just says, "You never owe me any explanations, Mila. And you never have to be afraid of me. There's nothing you could tell me that could scare me away."

He talks like that. Maybe it's a little weird because we *still* do not cuddle or hold hands or use pet names or refer to each other as girlfriend or boyfriend. If I want to be kissed by Christian, I have to initiate it. He never says he loves me.

I don't care. I don't need him to say, "I love you." What he says tonight is better.

"I will *never* be on anyone's side but yours."

I tell him the whole story, and I know he's not angry with me, but fury grows on his face as he learns that not only was I assaulted, but I was kicked off the expedition team because of it. As he ruminates over what happened, I realize I'm more shaken up than I knew, and the rest of the evening is spent in quiet distress. I don't want to talk anymore. He doesn't want to play his violin. Neither of us wants to watch a show or order take-out. We just stay up late together, eventually retiring to my sofa, where I finally feel too defeated to do anything but lean my head against his shoulder.

"Do you have to leave?" I say.

"Do you want me to *stay*?" he says with a little surprise in his voice.

He's never stayed at my place overnight. I hardly ever go to his at all. I have no idea what him staying will mean for us. But tonight, I'm willing to take a chance.

"I don't feel safe here alone."

"Your apartment has security staff."

"My *mind* isn't safe."

He hums like he's not happy with that. "I don't want you to rely on me to serve as your shield. Especially not from yourself. You don't need me."

This characterization chafes at me, and I'm reproachful in

my response. "Christian, you've been telling me for *years* that you're mine to do whatever I want with. You said I couldn't scare you away."

He has an excellent neutral expression, but there's a quick flash in his eyes—the slightest break at that. He doesn't want to turn me down, and it makes me feel *powerful* to know I can read him like this. I bet I'm the only person in the world who can do that.

"You can't. And I am," he says with a low, wavering voice.

"Then *stay*," I say with a touch of force I've never heard in my voice ever. "I don't *feel* like being alone."

His face finally relaxes, but then he frowns again. "Here?" He points at the sofa. "Or—?" He nods toward the hall that leads back to my bedroom.

He's never seen my bedroom.

"Here," I say, and he reaches for my shoulder and nudges me back toward him until I'm resting with my ear against his chest and his arm is around my back.

I'm not touchy-feely. Hardly anyone hugs me. Christian and I don't hug. But this feels right, and I manage to fall asleep. We have coffee together the next morning. Christian comes back the next night, and we sleep on my sofa again, and that's what happens every night until Bray is dead.

The official ruling is suicide, and the case is barely investigated. The guy was humiliated and fired. He left a note saying he couldn't handle being known as a sexual predator for all eternity. Shot himself with a handgun.

But I know it wasn't suicide because the night Bray supposedly kills himself, I can't get in touch with Christian for hours. I wonder if maybe he's tired of sleeping on my couch. Then he shows up to my apartment with a duffel bag of clothes and blood on his hands.

Actual blood.

He washes it off in my kitchen sink, and we have a short and useful conversation about the situation. He says, "Does this bother you?"

Did Bray deserve to live forever as a predator? Would anyone in the immortal community ever have served justice to him? Would I ever have felt safe knowing he was still alive? My ethics shift like gears changing on a bicycle, but I feel fine.

"No," I say.

Then after he dries his hands, I kiss him. We haven't kissed since before the assault, but if I'm leaving some part of myself behind tonight, I want to be closer to someone who understands. I take him to my bedroom for the first time.

It's not for sex.

He doesn't say I love you.

I do not want him to call me his girlfriend.

I am aware that this is not normal.

But he sleeps with me in my bed that night, and after that, he sleeps with me whenever I ask him to. I think my relationship with Christian is far better than any normal girl's relationship with her normal boyfriend. Who needs a boyfriend when you can have a guy who would kill for you instead?

5.

CHRISTIAN

2076 CE Earth

Immortality cheats us out of any possibility of a peaceful death. Doomed death is the price we pay for immortality. You live forever until you die horribly.

Mila says everything comes to an end, and the important thing is to do something worthwhile with the time you have. But Mila is an optimist by nature. Not that she would tell you that. She wouldn't. She might not even *know* it. Mila doesn't see herself clearly yet.

I see her, though. When Mila wants something, she pursues it stubbornly and persistently. She knows that if she works hard enough for long enough, eventually she will outsmart the fools trying to outwit her and get what she wants.

That is why being sexually assaulted and then kicked off the expedition team to Kepler doesn't sink her into a deep depression. It only makes her start thinking of creative ways to get back on that team. That is not a pessimist's perspective. That is an optimist. That is a fighter.

That is powerful.

But me? I am a pessimist by nature. Truly. Maybe it's what happens when you are born a savant. I've been the world's best violinist since before I became immortal. I was being praised as a child for accomplishing things other humans couldn't have accomplished in a mortal lifetime. Or maybe even an immortal lifetime. I never needed a big dream to go after. I never had to work for anything. My standards were set so high from the beginning that the only thing the world could do is disappoint me.

And it has. At seventy-two-years-old, I still have a perpetually young, optimally fit body and the mental elasticity of a twenty-seven-year-old. But I've had decades to observe all the scummy things humans do to each other. All I can say about humanity these days is that I'm looking forward to getting the hell out of Dodge—with Mila—and moving on to some other planet where, hopefully, we'll meet a more evolved species.

In the meanwhile, I'm biding my time, trying to avoid sheer boredom. Music helps with this, as does spending time with Mila. When music makes me weary and Mila is unavailable, I have Zaden and Phelps, the stooges who have remained loyal to me throughout the years.

I do not understand why they still follow me around. Zaden calls me his "best friend." What does this mean? Does it mean that he would kill for me? Take a bullet for me? Value me above all others? I don't think so. Zaden is married to a saggy sixty-five-old mortal. He *must* value her more than he values me. There's no other reason a guy with a twenty-seven-year-old body would go to bed every night with a woman more than twice his physical age.

But Zaden serves as my manager, and I pay him well to book my venues, protect my "brand," and make sure my work schedule never conflicts with the things I want to do with Mila. So maybe by "best friend," what he really means is "best employer." I understand that kind of exchange. I value him as one of my best service providers. The 'Z Howls broke up decades ago—crunk pop fans are fickle—but classical music never goes out of style. Without Zaden, I wouldn't have had the motivation to keep giving concerts.

Same with Phelps, though Phelps does not refer to me as a "friend." He calls me his "biggest pain in the ass." Which makes sense because he's the one who travels with me. He fights the sound engineers about how exactly the mics need to be set up, ensures that I have fresh food for dinner, and tells the stage managers that no, Christian Godric does not make "final remarks" after a show.

I probably am the biggest pain in his ass, and Phelps relieves the stress I cause him with a steady diet of young mortal girlfriends, usually between twenty-five and forty-five years of age. Which he says makes *him* the not-creepy one of the three of us. He's not entirely wrong. Last week, when Phelps picked up two twenty-two-year-old girls—mere *children* compared to us in actual age—I was far less disgusted than when Zaden told me he and his senior citizen wife are still having sex.

Grotesque.

But in any case, Zaden and Phelps are both useful minions. Therefore, I go out with them occasionally and tolerate the fact that they both think *I'm* the one with the bizarre love life.

"Don't you want a family, Chris?" Zaden asks one night when we're out getting drinks. I do not like being called "Chris," but he always thinks I'm joking when I say that. "You and Mila could have had kids by now. You could have grandkids."

I scoff at the thought. "Mortal children? Why would I want that?"

Zaden himself is why I don't want children, by the way. He had two children years ago with his mortal wife. One is now estranged because the ungrateful whelp thinks it is morally wrong to be immortal. As if Zaden had a choice with that. The other died young in a freak car accident.

"What *I* don't understand is how you've stayed abstinent all these years," Phelps says. "The sexual tension between you and that woman is thick as fog. If I were you, I'd want to cut that like a—"

"*Fog* is not that thick," I say, cutting off whatever lewd thing he was planning to say. "And I am insulted that you think my connection with Mila is anything that could so easily dissipate."

Phelps thwacks me on the back—another familiar gesture I scowl at—and Zaden laughs into his beer. But they don't understand. Mila and I are not some stupid sugary romance. I have far too much respect for her to push her in any direction, especially physically speaking, and I wouldn't want to do that anyway. The tension between us is tangible, and it gives us both something to hold onto. I have wanted her from the beginning. She seems to want me just as much. Neither of us trusts anyone else. The balance is perfect.

This doesn't mean that tension isn't going to snap one day, but it's the opposite of immortal death. We have all the time in the world to wind tighter and tighter around each other. When even one of those coils springs loose, it is an *exquisite* pleasure. The day the whole thing snaps will be a spectacular inevitability.

And I'm not going to rush it, and I don't want to control it. Mila is smart, beautiful, capable, and entirely unpredictable.

Zaden and Phelps cannot possibly understand what it is like when a woman like that kisses you because she is *thirsty*.

Anyway, sex will be ruined for me if it turns out to be more about desire fulfillment than the pain-pleasure of anticipation. I don't get anything from simply fulfilling a desire. I know because the night I killed the man who hurt Mila, I felt nothing. No remorse. No release. No relief. Only a sense of having completed a necessary task.

I was worried about how Mila would perceive what I had done, but she saw it the same way I did. Mila and I, we're in this for the climbs, not the hunts. But if knocking out a natural predator is what it takes to get to the next peak, so be it.

The kill made us closer.

Still, Mila doesn't know exactly who she is yet, and I hate how her employer treats her. The goddess continues all her research about Kepler alone, in her free time. In the meanwhile, she becomes the most important member of ImmortalSpace's grounded mission control team, and yet, every time she requests to be put back on the Kepler expedition team, her request is denied.

ImmortalSpace sells thousands of civilian tickets for the Eden Immortality Spacecraft, which will launch for Kepler in 2085. I secure my own ticket easily. Then Zaden's wife dies of cancer, and Phelps never could keep a girlfriend, and they, too, secure spots on the Eden Immortality. But Mila tries to buy a civilian ticket, and ImmortalSpace rejects her application.

I want to fix it for her—I have some clout with some people in high places who wear their association with people like me as a badge of high culture. But I don't offer, and I know she wouldn't let me anyway. It's one thing for me to avenge her after a man assaults her. It's another to make the enemies she needs to defeat disappear.

Mila wants those battles for herself.

But immortal or not, I am human, and I am therefore fallible. The hardest thing I ever have to do is watch her struggle for a place she deserves more than anyone on a spaceship to a planet that should be hers.

"What happens if you don't get in?" I ask her one time while we are alone together. I am rubbing her feet while she reads new reports about Kepler from her laptop on the sofa in her condo. Foot rubbing is one of the small intimacies she allows casually these days. Progress.

"If I don't get in, I don't get in," she says, but her brow is knit together, and I can see wheels turning in her mind. Not getting in is not an option.

Now, if she somehow *doesn't* make it onto that ship, I will not be going either. Period. But she thinks it's cute when I'm nonchalant about these things, and it fits the game we're playing better.

"Guess I'll send you a postcard when I get there."

"You do that," she says because she knows I'm lying. But then she does one of those things that makes my life less boring because of her. "I have a new plan, though, and there's something I need you to do."

I stop rubbing her feet. I am *always* waiting for moments like these, when she finally figures out that I'm hers to do anything she wants with. *Always.*

"And that is?"

"ImmortalSpace is hosting a fancy ribbon-cutting gala in the spring before the expedition team heads up to the orbital dock to start prepping the Eden Immortality for launch.

Black tie only."

I'm puzzled as to what she could possibly need from me related to a gala. Mila and I rarely go out in public together. If we're together, it's nearly always at her place. We like our privacy.

"Do you want me to play at the event?" I ask.

Her eyes flicker down and up again, her eyelashes brushing the air in a coy move she's never pulled with me before. Then she scoots around until she is in my lap with her arms around my neck.

Seventy years of perpetual youth and beauty, and Mila still mostly only wears jeans and t-shirts that aren't too tight. She has the body to get anything she wants—especially with me—but I've never seen her try it before. Not even with me.

Until now. This time, she kisses me like she wants to persuade. It's silly on one level because there is nothing I wouldn't give her if she asked, but I'm on board if she wants to make this our new thing. She's got my brain so dangerously fried by the time she pulls her lips away from mine that I tense up from the loss. The word "more" is on the tip of my tongue.

"Sorry," she whispers while I fight my own physiology.

"What do you … want?" I manage to say between staggered gasps for air.

"Be my date to the party."

I am so surprised by the innocence of her request that I don't say "yes" right away. Then she starts kissing me again, and I manage to choke out "why?" between more ragged breaths.

"I want—" she is *good* at this new persuasion "—to use you—" (very good) "—to make Silvey jealous."

"It's on my calendar," I say immediately.

Thereafter, the evening is one of those pleasures that is so exquisite I *almost* suggest sex. I narrowly avoid the slip, content simply to stay the night and continue caressing her as we begin to drift to sleep in her bed.

"Christian?" she says drowsily, while my lips chase the moonlight glowing on her bare shoulder.

"Hmm?"

"I love you."

I linger on a line of freckles near her neck. What is love? Is it when you value someone more than anyone else? When you would kill for them? When you would die for them? Or is it more like when you trust someone to hold the most vulnerable parts of you? When you trust them to keep you whole as you fall apart?

She twists to look back at me. "I wanted you to know. In case you have to see me do something … intimate … with Silvey. Is that okay?"

"Is that the plan? To seduce Silvey into putting you back on the team?"

She sighs. "Do you know he still thinks I'm some kind of administrative assistant? He never remembers my name. Not after all those years. But he has the power to put me back on that team."

I bite her shoulder while I consider this. Sink my teeth in slow enough not to hurt her but firm enough to leave a little mark. Mila shouldn't have to resort to this to get what she wants, but I approve of dirty tactics. She needs to understand all the ways she can have power, not just the intellectual ones.

"Are you angry at me?" she asks. "Are you going to respect me less?"

"If you have to sleep your way onto that ship?"

She blushes. "I'll *flirt* my way onto the ship. I'm not

having sex with that swine. But I mean, are you angry at me for loving you?"

My real opinion is that most people use the words "I love you" as bondage. They say it when they're afraid of losing someone they need. They expect you to say it back, not because you do love them, but because you are obligated either to reciprocate or end the relationship.

But that's not how things are between Mila and me. We're bonded so much tighter than a few words could possibly make us. The verbal confirmation isn't grating the way I always thought it would be. Maybe I simply couldn't say it first because I didn't want to obligate Mila to anything.

I pull the covers over us both and tuck her back against me. "I love you more, Mila."

"It's not a competition," she says.

"I know," I say.

"I'm not going to have sex with him."

"I know."

"If I do, it's not because I love him."

I bite her shoulder again. I'm less gentle, and she whimpers, but when I stop, she says, "No. Do it again. Leave real marks. I want him to know I don't belong to him."

"You will *never* be his," I say, going to work seriously on her request. We turn from exquisite pleasure to exquisite pain, and if the tension between us was high before, it is off the charts by sunrise. Mila says she is late to work and kicks me out without even letting me make a cup of coffee.

It isn't desire fulfillment, but I don't mind.

I never mind.

Mila Hildebrand is always worth the wait.

6.

MILA

The ship leaving for *my* planet is scheduled to depart in less than a decade. The expedition team has grown. It is now a crew of more than two-hundred and fifty immortals. I am still the most qualified person in the world to deserve a place on that crew, and I can't even secure a *civilian* ticket for the Eden Immortality.

I am desperate. That is the only reason I do what I do now. And I hate myself for it. I hate myself for renting a dozen James Bond-style movies so that I can study what exactly a woman *does* to use sex appeal to get a man like Jared Silvey to do what you want him to do.

I hate myself for watching a hundred YouTube hair and makeup tutorials, and I hate myself worse for ultimately deciding that I am so woefully bad at both that I need hired help. I schedule hair and makeup appointments for the morning of the gala at a spa one of Christian's friend's girlfriends recommends. The receptionist says, "oh, is this for a wedding?" and I almost cancel on the spot.

I hate that the designer heels I purchase cost almost

five-hundred dollars, and I hate that I'm so clumsy in them that I have to put them on every night after I get home from work and practice walking. I hate that after an exhausting day in a row of expensive boutiques, I still don't have a dress. I hate hiring a fashion designer (who knows one of Christian's other friends) to make me a dress meant to tempt.

I hate how ugly and awkward that first appointment with the designer makes me feel. The guy is an Italian who goes only by his first name, Guasparre, and I've barely said hello before he makes me strip down and stand on a pedestal in a room with a three-way mirror. He compliments my facial structure but tuts disapprovingly while he takes my measurements.

"Is there something wrong?" I ask, thinking that maybe there is something horribly disfigured about my body. Not that many people have seen me this bare. A few doctors? Christian, but not to this extent.

Guasparre flicks his fingers at my hip. "How can you dress *this* body in cotton underwear you purchased from Amazon?"

At least my actual body isn't disfigured, though, and the prescription Guasparre writes for new underwear is maybe the only thing I like about this whole ordeal. I order all of it online, and it's the first clothing I wear that ever makes me feel sexy. Also, Guasparre is much happier with me the day I come to pick up the dress. I understand why. The dress is plunging-neckline and curve-hugging, and it fits so tight that I need silky lingerie or you'd see every line underneath.

I do not end up hating Guasparre.

Christian meets me at my condo the day of the gala, and I am in my master bathroom, attempting to zip up the dress when he arrives.

"Just come back here," I call to him. "I need help anyway."

He enters the bathroom, and the look on his face when he sees me for the first time is awful. It's like he just smelled his dinner, and it's all rotten.

"It's terrible, isn't it?" I can barely catch his eye in the mirror, I am so mortified. "I feel so cheap. I hate this hairdo, and I don't know *why* that makeup artist thought I needed so much eyeliner, and—"

He pulls a small black velvet pouch out of his tuxedo pocket and hands it to me before neatly stepping behind my shoulders.

"I thought maybe you'd like this, but you already look perfect," he says while he zips up my dress. "I'm afraid it's going to ruin the effect."

I remove a gorgeous gold necklace with a spectacular, diamond-studded star pendant from the pouch, and the light seems to catch every diamond at once.

It's cliché, but I gasp anyway. I know what this is. This is a reminder. I'm doing this because I'm trying to touch the stars.

"You hate it," he says.

"It's the only thing I *want* to wear."

His expression softens in the mirror, and when I catch his eye, he smiles. "Maybe after this is all over," he says. He takes the pendant back and clasps the chain around my neck, sweeping his fingers along my collarbone to arrange the necklace just right on my skin.

When he's done, I look at myself with Christian standing behind me. My eyes are the same shade of red as before, and I *do* love the necklace, but everything else …

Christian slides his hands down my shoulders and around to the curves of my waist and hips in a sensual move that makes me shiver. "Silvey isn't going to know what hit him.

What do you need me to do tonight?"

Apparently, he likes the dress.

"Exactly what you just did," I say. "And kiss me? Act like I'm the lover you can't wait to take home? Especially when I might be in Silvey's line of vision? Make him want to be you."

He sweeps aside my hair and leans in to kiss my neck, and with one of his hands still curled around my hip, it looks sexy in the mirror.

"How's that?" Christian murmurs.

It makes me sad to answer "perfect."

I time our arrival so that we're "fashionably" late to the hotel ballroom where the gala is being held. It's a full cocktails, dinner, dancing thing, and there's a set of stairs leading down from the lobby to the reception hall where guests are mingling when we arrive.

Eyes are on me the moment we make our way down those stairs. I have never worn anything that made me feel more exposed, but at least I've gotten good enough at walking in these shoes that my feet aren't going to be bleeding at the end of the night. I scan for Silvey and spot him immediately. He's in the middle of the room.

Christian—who is doing a very good job keeping me hanging off his arm like I'm his hired escort—pulls me toward him, kisses behind my ear, and whispers, "Those stares are good stares, Mila."

"Those people probably don't even recognize me," I whisper back.

"Who's the woman with Silvey?" Christian asks. "Red hair? Long black dress?"

I see her. That's Jennifer Silvey. "Wife." I make an effort

to catch Silvey's eye from all the way across the room, and Guasparre's dress does wonders. Silvey sees me looking at him. I don't think I can pull off a wink, but I can pull off a smile while Christian tugs me closer.

"Looks like this is game on," Christian murmurs.

"Yep," I say, turning back to him and throwing my arms around his neck like maybe I'm a little tipsy. Then I kiss him, and he does a good job helping me make that cringy little display of affection showy, allowing his hands to slide too low down my back.

He gives my lips another peck. "Congratulations. Silvey's got his eyes all over you."

Success, then. I throw my shoulders back—confidence, Mila!—and remind myself it's only a game. A dirty trick I'm playing on a man who hasn't given me nearly the respect I deserve. "Let's make our way over there."

I've never enjoyed a cocktail hour. I don't like mingling or small talk. And I know this isn't something Christian enjoys either, but we've agreed that for this to work, we need to work the room. So we get drinks, and then I start butting into one conversation after another.

"Oh, Billie! I love your dress!" I tell a woman who works with me on mission control. I'm lying through my teeth; her dress is hideous.

"Hey, Sam! Read that report. Solid work!" I tell a man who works in interplanetary environmental science. It was terrible work on a subject I had already written a *much* better report about myself.

"Peter, I heard you got that promotion you wanted. Congratulations!" I say to one of our aerospace engineers.

Peter didn't deserve the promotion. It should have gone to a young woman named Gage, who makes me think of me thirty years ago.

This goes on and on, and every time I make a stop, the person I speak to acts the same as the last. They look at me like they can't remember who I am. Then they do a double-take, say, "*Mila?*" and, depending on how gauche they are, they either make a comment about my looks or my date. "I hardly recognized you in that dress!" or "I didn't know you had a boyfriend!"

It's not awful, except for the two times when someone says, "Mila *Hildebrand?* I didn't know you were even planning to be here tonight. You're not on the crew."

The first time it happens, it's Wren Augur. Christian's hand tightens where he has it on my waist. I smile and say, "Oh, I'm just being supportive."

The second time, it's Delphine Vardelle, and I bite back.

"The ship hasn't launched *yet,*" I say.

She narrows her eyes, and I think about how conniving she is. "I'm aware of that," she snaps. Then she tilts her head toward Silvey and says something unexpected. "But, I hear Silvey has a few *personal* guest spots left to fill."

I don't quite understand what's going on here. Is she on to me?

Delphine smiles tightly. "You know, Silvey *still* can't remember my name. He thinks I'm Wren's secretary, and she's on a power trip, even though almost everything she tells him comes from something *you* wrote or researched." She lifts one perfectly plucked eyebrow delicately. "Don't think you're the only one who's ever been mistaken for being just some dumb hussy, Mila. This company is full of sexist pigs. *I* hope Silvey falls all over you."

"Looks like you have an ally," Christian says as we walk away. "But the rest of those fools are disposable."

"I'll remember that for when I'm the ruler of the Eden Immortality," I say sarcastically.

"Oh, don't worry. If you don't, I will," he says. He does not sound at all sarcastic.

By the time we get to Captain Silvey, I'm warmed up and ready to make my big play. I pull Christian toward Silvey like I'm trying to get to someone *other* than the captain, and when I get close enough, I let my feet slip so that I bump Silvey. It's just the right angle to make my cocktail slosh on his arm.

"Excuse me," he says, but not in a nasty voice at all, and I turn on an enormous smile and start brushing the alcohol off his sleeve.

"*Oh*, Captain Silvey—" I fake-giggle for-real nervously "—I am *so* sorry." I hand my wine glass to Christian, look adoringly into my "boyfriend's" eyes, and say, "I'm going to need more wine, please?"

Christian kisses me right in front of Silvey, then smiles at him like a cocky bastard. "Certainly, darling," he says.

Silvey's wife is nowhere to be seen, so when Christian saunters away to retrieve drink refills, this leaves me alone with the captain, whom I've clearly distracted.

I start fake-fawning all over Silvey. "Is your tux okay?" I hold onto his arm like I need to see his tux to make sure nothing stained. It didn't. The splash wasn't *that* impressive. But my plan is still working. Silvey's eyes rake down that plunging neckline.

He chuckles and pats my arm. "It's nothing at all!" he says. "Do I know you? I feel like you should be familiar."

Of course, he can't remember me.

"I'm Mila," I say, adding a little breathlessness to my voice. "But I know who *you* are. You're the man who's leading the Kepler expedition. I was on your team forever ago, remember?"

He nods like he's trying to remember, but he doesn't. I'm sure of it. Or he's too busying lusting over me to put effort into remembering me. His eyes are nowhere near mine.

I fight the urge to squirm.

"Right … and now you're in … um …?"

"Mission control." I still have my hand on his arm, and I'm smiling at him like I'm in love. "It was *so* sweet of you to transfer me after that whole mess with Bray."

"Ahh, I remember now!" (He doesn't.) "And, how's mission control treating you, Mila?" (He doesn't care.)

I think he's already decided he wants me, though. He's stroking my hand and smiling like he loves how much power he has over me.

I vow to myself that one day, he will have *nothing* over me. But I start chatting with him about mission control and how *thrilling* it is to work *anywhere* at ImmortalSpace and how *proud* I am to do work that's going to help *his* team. Then, when I can see Christian coming back with those drinks, I say, "I have to tell you, though, Captain Silvey, at first I was relieved to be away from all that drama, but now I'm just *heartbroken* not to be going on the mission. I can't believe that after you and the crew head up to the ship to prep it, I'll *never* get to see you again."

I'm laying it on thick and sticky, and this shouldn't work because it's that corny, but I think I'm pulling off a honey trap. Silvey definitely doesn't look like a man who's thinking with his brain right now.

"I don't suppose we could talk about it?" I say, batting my eyelashes like the Bond girls in the oldest movies I watched would have done.

He smiles at me like a creepy old man would do in any era. "We can find time to talk. Do you need a drink?"

"Oh, no, my boyfriend is getting one for me," I tell him, and right on cue, Christian is there, handing me a drink.

"Thanks for taking care of her for me, captain," he says as he's slipping his arm around me again, then wrapping his hand around my rib cage. His fingers just barely graze the swell of my chest, and I'm glad I brought the right accomplice with me tonight. Silvey's eyes jealously follow everything Christian's hands do.

Perfect.

Silvey clears his throat, "Well, uh, Mila, why don't you stop by my office Monday after work so we can talk about the mission?"

I bite my lip. "I usually work pretty late. How late is too late for me to stop by?"

Silvey's pupils have dilated so much his eyes are merely a ring of red. He licks his tooth. "Oh, I'll be around." Then he nods at Christian. "Looks like someone else wants you right now."

"I do," Christian says, without any wit in his voice, and when I look, I see that his face has tensed up. It's unexpected. I suddenly don't think Christian is acting anymore. Did something in all this bring out some kind of possessiveness in him? I hope not. I don't have the energy to deal with drama from someone I truly care about.

I let Christian whisk me away from Silvey, and to reward him for tolerating this, I spend the rest of the evening mostly paying attention just to him. It's good for the act. I catch

Silvey looking at me at least four times during dinner, and he's so caught up that he manages to steal a dance later. Christian is very sullen about that.

"I hate these people." He growls when I'm back in his arms. "You should be dominating them. They should be worshiping at your feet."

"I can't *dominate* any of them if I'm not on that ship when it launches."

"Yeah, well, you definitely secured your ticket," he says darkly. "All you have to do now is keep flirting with Silvey until launch."

Until launch.

That's almost a decade away. Why didn't that part of this occur to me? I'm not going to be able to keep up a stupid *tease* for that long. This is going to be a real affair. With a man I hate. For *years*.

"Hey," Christian says. "I'm sorry. It's okay. We'll get our revenge one day. Launch isn't that far away."

I feel dizzy and sick. How did it come to this?

"Mila?"

"I need to go home," I say.

7.

CHRISTIAN

Mila is beautiful no matter what she wears, but the dress that the designer made for her is stunning, and she wears it like a queen. It's the easiest thing in the world to have my hands all over her at the ribbon-cutting gala. But by the time the evening is over, I can tell she's not feeling it anymore.

"It's late," she says as we walk up the steps together to her condo.

"Does that mean you don't want me to stay?" I ask.

Her shoulders droop, and I take her keys from her, open the door for her, and steer her to her bedroom. Mila's eyeliner is smudged below her eyes, the curls in her hair are hanging loose, and her face is drawn so tight, I'm sure she has a migraine.

We're barely in her bedroom before she starts tearing at that dress and panicking over her inability to get it off on her own.

"Hey, hey, let me help," I say, and I unzip it for her. The dress falls to the floor, leaving Mila in heels and lingerie. I have never seen her quite like this, and I always thought

53

lingerie would be sexy on Mila, but this is not sexy. It is not sexy to watch someone you love in absolute misery.

"I hate *all* of this," she says as tears threaten to spill from her eyes.

I want to tell her it's okay again, but the truth is, it's not. It's not okay that she had to resort to this. She deserves to feel beautiful just because. She deserves to be recognized for how valuable she is. She should *never* be made to feel cheap.

Her face twists up, and she hurries to the bathroom and slams the door behind her. I try to get in when I hear her vomiting, but she's locked the door. Again and again, she throws up until she's dry heaving and weeping, and all I can do is lean against the wall and wait.

When she's done, she crawls into bed without even bothering to change into pajamas and buries herself under the duvet.

"You should go," she says into her pillow.

Normally, if she said something like that, I would go, but this time, instead of leaving at her command, I lose the tux and strip down to underclothes to make things even. I don't want any part of me staying with her tonight to make her feel like I have more power than she does. I don't. We are not equals. No matter what she thinks, it is my world that revolves around her, not the other way around.

"I don't need you to protect me," she says when I climb into bed with her.

"This isn't me protecting you," I tell her. "This is me not abandoning you."

A sob wracks through her, and I'm not sure why that made her more upset until she says, "I'm going to have to sleep with *him* … and probably other things. And *then* you'll want to abandon me."

I kiss her shoulder. "Bullshit."

She turns to look at me with completely red, bloodshot eyes. "It's *not* bullshit, Christian! This is the worst thing I've ever done. I've *never* felt so ashamed."

I kiss the corner of her mouth, then the opposite corner, then the tip of her nose, her forehead, the tiny, tiny mole on her left cheek, and between those kisses, I tell her what she needs to know.

"None of this is fair, Mila. You shouldn't have to do any of it. You shouldn't have to sink to their level. But it is bullshit for you to think I would ever abandon you. As long as I live, there will *always* be someone who understands you and respects you."

She seems to relax a little, but she sighs and says, "If you want, we could … before I have to start this … affair. So he's not …"

I kiss her again—a real kiss on the mouth. Though I have to keep it short because she's been crying too hard to be able to breathe through her nose right now.

"Nothing you do with Silvey is going to be anything like anything you ever do with me. And I don't want to do anything with you that you don't *truly* want to. Just for you, you know? I want you to be a *selfish* lover with me."

She sniffs. "What if one day, I decide that what *I* want is to know what *you* want?"

"Then one day, you'll find out," I tell her. "But not before we get rid of Silvey." The tone of my voice darkens. "His days are numbered."

She laughs. "How exactly are we going to get rid of him?"

"Poison. Stabbing. Strangling." I yawn. "I don't know. I'll think of something suitably creative. I believe there are several excellent ways to dispose of an enemy in space. Many involving airlocks." She knows better than to think I'm joking, so I kiss her once again to lighten the mood. "And once we're done with him, *you* shall rule the universe."

She copies my yawn. "When I rule the universe, I shall make you my top general."

"Lovely, Empress," I say. "When shall we begin making plans?"

"Tomorrow," she says. And then she falls asleep.

I will never abandon Mila, but the next decade does change her. She spends several weeks flirting with Silvey at work. She changes her wardrobe and her hair and her schedule for him. She dangles him on a string, and he falls for all of it.

I continue to tell her that my opinion of her is not going to change, but the more she sees of him, the less she wants to see of me. I ignore the prick of jealousy, but it stings anyway, especially the night she finally gets word that she is an official member of the crew.

She comes to my place that evening—a rarity for us—and when she shows up, her hair is messed up, her dress is wrinkled, and I can smell men's cologne on her. She doesn't want to talk; she asks me to play my violin for her. She sits in a chair near a window and stares out at the moon.

"What are you thinking about?" I ask her after I finish the first song.

"What it would be like to live on the moon," she says, and I recall the first conversation I had with her. "But I don't like being alone with myself anymore."

There are no tears in her eyes while she speaks. I haven't seen her cry since the night of that party. But somehow, this doesn't feel better. Something sacred has been violated here, and it isn't just the body of a goddess. Silvey's got his claws in Mila's soul, and I think it's poisoning her.

A month or so later, she shuttles up with the rest of the crew to the station where the Eden Immortality is docked in Earth's orbit, and I am left behind. Civilian passengers won't board for six more years.

So now, when I see Mila, it is virtually, and I can't tell if she has hardened as much as it seems. Our conversations are stiff, and she's all business, except that she doesn't want to talk about her work or the four-thousand-year trip we're about to take or what we'll do when we get to Kepler. Which really only leaves, "how are things on Earth?" (the same as they were yesterday), "how was your last concert?" (good as always), and "don't forget to pack X" (that, at least, is helpful).

A few weeks after she leaves Earth, we have a call that lasts fifteen minutes before we get to this:

Me: "So."

Her: Nothing.

Me: Nothing.

Her: "Christian, I think we need to take a break."

Me: "From each *other?*"

"It's just, Silvey is even stupider than I thought, and Wren's got him in her back pocket, but she barely knows what she's doing, and she still hasn't acknowledged that I'm on the crew at all, even though she's still stealing all my research. And Silvey doesn't even see any of it happening, and he asks me to get him coffee and screen his calls, and that's between when he's trying to get me to—"

I cringe. I don't want to hear the rest, and she doesn't want to say it.

She sighs so loud the audio picks up static. "Look, I'm dealing with a lot up here, and I only survive it by pretending it's not happening. But I can't pretend it away when I talk to you. We'll have thousands of years together after we launch. Until then, I don't think I can do this."

I understand, but the logistics of what she wants are unclear. "So, you want to break up for six years?"

"I want to not *video chat* with you every day for six years," she says. "If you want, we can still talk when I'm feeling up for it. And I get a vacation on Earth every four months. We can spend those together as long as we don't have to spend them doing anything that reminds me of Silvey."

I agree to the pseudo-break, but it leaves me seething inside. This is Silvey's fault. Silvey is the reason Mila doesn't want to talk to me every day anymore. I start thinking it's not good enough just to dispose of him. I want to punish him for what he's done to her. I want him to suffer. And there's an unjustness even to that because I know Mila is the one who should get to destroy him one day, not me.

So I will wait.

But in the meanwhile, I have more alone time than I've ever had. So I use the last few years I have left on Earth to do two things. The first is selfish. It's finding a master who can teach me how to make my own stringed instruments. It's not like we're going to Kepler without any technology. The ship is built around a huge, self-contained biosphere, and it has vacuum-sealed storage chambers so that things we take with us, like my violin, won't degrade quickly over time. Still, we don't know exactly what materials will be available when we get to Kepler. I'll need to be a master to use those materials to make new instruments after we land.

The second thing I do is about Mila. She's always worked

so hard, and she hardly ever does leisure. So I plan our vacations to make sure she won't regret not having seen something important on Earth. We go to Bali, then St. Petersburg, then South Africa, then Patagonia.

I perform private concerts for her in special places on our trips. One time, I take her to an abandoned cathedral in Rome. Another time, I play for her in the middle of Tiananmen Square, surrounded by thousands of tourists. These things are important to me. Mila doesn't talk about Silvey while she's with me on those vacations, but he's always at the top of my mind. I need to make sure she sees me as an entirely different species from that guy. Playing my violin for her is one way I draw the distinction.

It's funny how these things go, but that time passes day by day, and soon enough, I'm on the ship with all the other civilians, settling in like passengers on a cruise. The Eden Immortality is the first of fifteen ships launching for a new planet, and the journey is an enormous commitment. We stay in Earth's orbit for two years to allow anyone who gets cold feet at the last minute to ditch and also to make sure no one forgot to pack something critical.

I see Mila from time-to-time while we're in orbit, but never for long. She doesn't feel she can end her affair with Silvey until we've left the solar system. But I'm a first-class passenger, and I have a cabin with a window view. I invite her to watch the launch with me from there, and she agrees. She meets me in my cabin for our very last look at our home planet Earth.

I am not without sensitivity to the gravity of the moment, but I watch Mila almost as much as I watch Earth while we depart. She looks different. Her sunshine-honey hair is styled. Guasparre is a passenger now, and I think he makes all Mila's clothing. She stands like she feels powerful and in control. But there's not a trace of the gentle smile that used to rest on her face when she was feeling content.

What did getting here cost her soul?

"Do you think we'll miss it?" she says.

"Earth? I don't think we'll know if we miss it until we're on Kepler."

Mila doesn't take her eyes off our home planet. "I bet we'll miss spring water for the next four thousand years. Recycled water never tastes right."

"We won't miss pollution," I say. "Or overpopulation. Or the commercialization of everything."

Earth is quickly becoming too small to see clearly. We're both quiet while we catch our last glimpse of the blue marble. We may return one day, but I feel in my gut that we're leaving forever.

Then Mila turns to me. We are both nearly eighty years old. We don't have wrinkles on our foreheads or saggy bellies. We don't have age spots or hair growing out of our ears. And yet, there is something about her face that looks older.

Mila never talks about what she has to do to keep Silvey happy. What does she do with him? Does it ever involve anything she wants? Does he even care about her needs, or is it all about him? I want to ask, but Mila hasn't kissed me since I boarded the Eden Immortality, and something is curdling in my brain over it.

Just then, though, she threads her fingers through mine. "At least I won't have to miss you," she says. "Thanks for not abandoning me."

I hold tight. "Never."

8.

MILA

2096 CE Eden Immortality Spacecraft

For the longest time, I thought if I could just get on the Eden Immortality Spacecraft, everything else I wanted would fall in line. I thought I could end my affair with Silvey. I thought I'd be folded into the crew. I didn't anticipate that I wouldn't be allowed to participate in meetings with the planetary research team that Wren Augur leads. I didn't expect hostility and whispers about how I slept my way onto this ship.

Who cares what I had to do to get onto this ship? So what if I'm on board as Silvey's "personal assistant?" They all know that I'm still more qualified than any of them to be here. And none of them had to go through the hell I did to get here.

I'm losing hours of sleep every night pouring over every report that comes in about Kepler from the telescopes and probes we've sent out, too. I'm the one filing memo after memo about my findings in the ship's logs, and the crew is using my memos. The planetary research team puts out a newsletter about new Kepler findings every week. The highlights of my memos are always in the newsletter, word-for-word, under Wren Augur's byline.

Silvey has no idea. Because he's an idiot. I may not be part of the planetary research team. Still, as Silvey's personal assistant, there are plenty of opportunities for me to watch him. He is a terrible leader. He promotes people who stroke his ego instead of promoting actually competent people. He barks orders and makes snap decisions based on his "gut."

I am constantly stunned at how often he is willing to ignore the flight officers, the aerospace engineers, the navigational technicians, the environmental control engineers, and the ship governance council. The trip from Earth to Kepler is going to take almost four-thousand years, and that's only if we can avoid major disasters that would throw us significantly off-course. We can't afford to make decisions based on anyone's "gut" when it comes to things like unexpected gravity fields that threaten to detour our trip or malfunctioning life support systems.

Maybe that's why a year after launch, I'm still engaging in an affair with him. Everyone knows about it. The crew knows. Silvey's wife knows. Christian knows. It's humiliating. I hate everything that goes on between Silvey and me, from the way he treats me when he's asking me to run errands for him to the way he treats me when he's unbuttoning his shirt in front of me. I'm disgusted with him for using me and disrespecting me, and I'm disgusted with myself for letting it happen. No, for *making* it happen.

But despite all that, I have Silvey's ear, and I'm good at putting ideas in it that he'll think are his. It is because of me that Silvey doesn't do anything we can't recover from in those first years. My judgments keep the ship from disaster, and I don't yet know how to claim more direct power from Silvey.

Maybe I'm waiting for something. Maybe Christian was right. I needed to change. I *still* need to change. I need more self-confidence. More self-respect. A strong enough spine to tell Silvey it's over and that he needs me as more than the girl who makes his coffee and relieves his stress.

I'm not there yet, though.

Perhaps I need to fight a smaller battle first.

I start working out a plan to expose Wren for the fraud she is. The cheating bitch has been relying on my work for decades now, and I should be the one in her place. Luckily, I'm not the only one who wants to see Wren taken down. Delphine is done with her, too. Ever since the ribbon-cutting gala, Delphine's been different with me. Not nicer exactly, but less biting. Less passive-aggressive.

I decide that a self-confident Mila would confront Delphine about the change and manipulate it to her advantage. So I stop by Delphine's private cabin one evening after Silvey is done with me. She opens the door and says, "Mila? What are you doing here?"

"I want to talk," I say.

She steps aside and motions for me to come inside. Her cabin is not nearly as nice as Silvey's penthouse suite or Christian's first-class cabin. Delphine has a futon, a few chairs, a coffee table, and a kitchenette. But I note that her cabin is still significantly better than the tiny closet with a bed and a sink that I have.

I sit down in one of her chairs and decide that one day, Silvey's suite will be mine.

"Coffee?" Delphine asks.

"Yes," I say because someone with confidence accepts

coffee from a frenemy.

She brings a cup to me. I take it and sip while she sits down in the other chair.

"So," she says.

I don't say anything yet. One thing I have gained from my time with Silvey is a sense of how powerful people get weaker people to talk. Silence is a motivator.

"I've meant to tell you, I like the new look," she says.

When I am not staying up late to work on the research I care about or serving as Silvey's eye candy, I spend my time perfecting my look. I have decided that physical appearance is as much a part of power as anything else, but it's an art. I've studied and practiced to become good at it over the last few years.

Delphine has gotten worse. Her eyeliner is a little smudged, and her lipstick looks uneven. Her blouse is too snug, and her hair is too thin for its length.

"You should try a bob," I say. "It would suit your facial structure nicely." But you can't say something like that and not add a compliment. "It would be cute on you."

I smile magnanimously at her while she touches her hair anxiously. I was far too socially awkward to have pulled this off when I first met Delphine.

But I've learned.

"How are things on the planetary research team?" I ask.

Delphine snorts into her coffee. "Awful. We've barely done anything useful for the last decade. Wren doesn't know where to go next with the research."

I say nothing. I am very aware of that. The thing is, we have a lot of information about Kepler. The team has done a lot of speculation about where we might land and where the best resources might be and what the climate might be like, but there's so much more to be done. So many details to fill in on the way to creating an entirely new civilization on an unexplored planet.

I notice that Delphine has a picture of herself and an old woman on a shelf.

"It's my mother," Delphine says. "She was still alive when we left. I had two mortal brothers who were taking care of her."

"My family had all passed," I say.

"I'm sorry."

"Personally, I think it's better this way," I tell her. "I didn't have any ties left to cut."

Delphine nods, and then we are both silent again. I relax into it, but she breaks the silence when it gets too awkward for her to handle. Precisely what I want.

"The navigation technicians are all pissed at Silvey. They say he nearly refused to redirect our course to avoid a collision with an asteroid."

"He did," I confirm. "I talked him into agreeing with them. I'm persuasive."

She laughs. "I don't know what you're planning with him, Hildebrand, but I'm glad he's got someone with some brains in his ear. Wish you were the one leading the planetary research team, though. Wren's a disaster. She's still directly quoting your reports like they're hers."

I am flattered at the way she said, "Hildebrand," and I barely resist cackling at her assessment of Wren. "I've been thinking of putting something bogus in my next report, just to throw her off," I admit.

Delphine's eyes light up. "Do it! Fabricate a false annual report and feed it to her for the big state of the ship thing coming up next month. Put something embarrassingly stupid in it. The team would kill to see her caught. They all know you're the one doing the work for her."

I scoff at the idea. "Knowing the way this ship works, she'd accuse me of sabotaging her, and I'd be the one in trouble."

Delphine sits forward all of a sudden. "So let *us* do it. Did you know Eldrye Dresden can hack into, like, anything? You write the report, finish it early, and let us handle the rest."

"You would do that?" I believe she would, but my challenge is meant to bolster her commitment.

Delphine meets my eyes with a fierce stare. "Wren has screwed me over for at least a dozen promotions. She never listens to any of my ideas, she constantly shuts me down, and she punishes me if I fight back. She thinks she knows who's loyal to her, but people change, and in the end, competence always wins over corruption."

"Okay, then," I say, and that's all I have to do. From there, I just continue exactly as I have for the next few weeks. I keep working hard. I keep writing solid reports with good information based on my own personal research of Kepler.

Then I sit at Silvey's right hand at the annual "state of the ship" meeting—to take notes, of course—and I listen as Wren gives the planetary research report, spouting off all kinds of stupid stuff that I never said. It's amazing. Everyone can tell that she's way off base, and she just keeps talking like she doesn't see people giving her funny looks.

It keeps going until Eldyre Dresden raises his hand to question something. "Excuse me, Doctor Augur, but did you just say the Kepler day is expected to be twice as long as an Earth day? Didn't we establish years ago that a Kepler day is only a minute or so shorter than an Earth day?"

Wren's face reddens while she looks through her notes

again. "Uh, no, I didn't say that," she says. "I said … 'The Kepler day is expected to be twice' … uh …"

She trails off.

Silvey leans toward me and lets his elbow brush mine. He does this. Acts like we're familiar, when really, he hardly knows anything about me. "Did that just happen?" he whispers like we're in on a joke together.

I don't respond. I'm busy watching Wren realize she's messed up. She flounders as she looks through the report she has been reading verbatim. Then Delphine asks her another question she can't answer. Then someone else on the team does the same. And I get to see all Wren's lies unravel as the team picks her apart like vultures and Silvey watches amused.

Until the end. When Delphine says, "Why don't you just admit that you've been stealing Mila Hildebrand's independent research for years, Wren? Because *you're* too incompetent to do your own job."

The meeting explodes. Wren starts spouting off denials. The team gets aggressive countering everything she says. People talk over each other. Silvey has to stand up and bang the table, and it's several minutes before everyone notices and shuts up.

Then Silvey turns his eyes on me. "Mila? Was that your report?"

I have the sense that for the very first time, he's seeing me a different way.

"I did write a report," I say, demurely, with my eyes down. "But it wasn't the one Wren just gave."

Eldrye Dresden pulls a folder out from below a stack of papers that have been sitting in front of him. "No. This is Mila's report. It's perfectly correct and extremely useful." He slides it over to Silvey, who picks it up and starts reading.

"We knew Wren was stealing Mila's research, so Dresden hacked the system and fabricated a false report under Mila's name," Delphine says. She is looking straight at Wren. "Doctor Augur is just so ignorant *she* couldn't tell the difference."

Silvey looks down at me and holds up the report. "Is this *yours*, Mila?"

I am not sure how this is going to go, but if there was ever a moment for me to take a stand, it's now. "Yes," I admit.

He nods. "Well. It looks like Wren Augur has a replacement."

I find Wren later in the women's bathroom. She's crying. I put a hand on her shoulder and notice that her blouse does *not* go with that skirt.

"Aww, don't be bitter, Wren," I whisper. "We're still all getting to Kepler the same way."

Wren doesn't even respond.

You would think that Silvey's interest in me would end as soon as he learns I have a brain. Unexpectedly, it doesn't. He finds a civilian he thinks is hot to take over for me as his personal assistant, and he doesn't ask me to run copies for him anymore, but now he shows up to the office I've taken over from Wren at least once a day.

"I need your secret brain, Mila," he starts saying. Then he asks for my opinion on whatever crisis he doesn't know how to handle. There's a shower of what looks like alien trash threatening to detour our trip. The navigation technicians think we should go around it. The pilots want to plow through it. What should we do? People in the second and third class cabins have been stealing from people in the first-class cabins. What should we do? The astronauts refuse to perform EVAs anymore unless they are given an additional day off for every ten days' work. What should we do?

I thought I had his ear before, but it only takes a year or so of this before I'm his right-hand advisor. I have no idea what his actual first and second mates do all day. Nothing useful, apparently. And I am soon so overworked both handling planetary research and making sure that I have enough information about everything else going on to help Silvey, that Silvey himself notices I'm exhausted.

Guess even he can take a hint. Or maybe when your lover falls asleep while you're in bed together for something other than sleep, you get more than a hint.

"What's going on?" Silvey asks me. Like he might almost be concerned. It's funny. I never enjoy anything we do together. He is crude, rough, and oblivious. I fake everything. But lately, he's had a few moments when he's been almost affectionate.

"I want to help you," I tell him honestly. I do. Because I don't want to *die* before I get to Kepler, and we will all surely die if I'm not helping Silvey. "But it's hard to stay on top of everything without any assistance."

Silvey says, "if I get you more assistance, will you be more awake the next time we're together?"

That's promising, so I lie to him. "Yes."

The next day, Silvey promotes me to chief executive officer and authorizes me to form subject matter expert teams for any problem I think we need to prepare for or deal with. I can assign anyone to an expert team, and no one except Silvey has veto power over my orders.

I ask Delphine to take over as the lead planetary researcher, and I go to work finding the best minds we have on this ship for everything else. Under my leadership, we have a dozen solid committees of competent experts who I trust within a few weeks. Problems come through me first, and they only get reported to Silvey if my teams can't solve them within forty-eight hours.

Silvey compliments me for my problem-solving and leadership abilities. He has more free time because of me, he says. People "bother" him less. But people bother *me* more, and Silvey is now jealous and possessive of me. The affair isn't just about sex for him anymore. Now he kisses me and wants to spend time together. He shows up at my cabin to chat. He asks me to stay the night in his. He invites me to go out with him.

"How well do you know Jennifer?" he asks one night while we're eating dinner together in one of the ship's little restaurants.

I had just been telling him about a problem I foresee coming with the produce supply. Our hydroponic farm is having a bad season thanks to an imbalance of nutrients in the water supply. The mistake was made by someone Silvey put in charge last year. I fired the guy last week and replaced him with a much smarter woman.

"Um, does Jennifer have expertise in hydroponics?" I ask. Maintaining a continual food supply is obviously a critical element of surviving a four-thousand-year space journey. I don't know why we're discussing Silvey's wife.

Silvey swallows down a huge chunk of plant-based Salisbury steak, covered in gravy. "Jennifer wants to be friends with you. She thinks that will make this—" he gestures between us with his fork "—easier for everyone."

"Your wife wants a relationship with your mistress," I say flatly.

Silvey smiles broadly. "Mila, honey, are terms like that

even relevant to immortals? Jennifer and I got married long before we took the virus. We'd known each other for two years. Had no idea that 'til death do we part' would be so far away. And I just don't see the point in any immortal committing to a relationship for life that isn't a little flexible."

Silvey's relationship with his wife is more than a little flexible. Jennifer has had her share of affairs, which I do not blame her for. And I don't really care what other people want to do with their relationships, but I'm already disgusted with myself for the interaction I have with Jared Silvey. I'm not looking to make it more permanent by adding his wife to the show.

"You're not still seeing that Christian guy, are you?" Silvey says. "I heard he'd hooked up with Wren Augur."

I am affirmatively not hungry now. "I'll think about it," I tell Silvey.

Silvey pats my hand. "That's my girl."

9.

CHRISTIAN

There are a couple thousand civilians on board the Eden Immortality, but just because we are civilians, doesn't mean we don't work. We all have a role to play. I give music lessons, direct a volunteer orchestra, and play concerts from time-to-time. Zaden is one of the ship's two DJs. Phelps works in logistics with resource distribution.

Because of this, news travels fast when there's a problem, and rumors spread rampantly. Within the first two decades of our trip, Captain Jared Silvey is the laughing stock of the ship, and everyone knows the person running the show is the CEO, Mila Hildebrand, Silvey's smexy mistress.

You got a problem? You go to Hildebrand, not Silvey. She gets shit done.

Silvey knows his place at the helm is at risk. You can tell by the way he starts appearing with Mila in public, acting like a power-hungry ape with his mate. More than once, I see him kiss her in public. More than once, I hear him talk about her in a degrading way when she's not there.

He wants to own her, not the other way around. He's

going to find out soon enough that no one owns Mila Hildeb-rand, but in the meanwhile, I'm a wreck over the whole thing. I find myself wanting to threaten Silvey and take him down myself. Forget punishment. I now imagine a bloody fight to the death. And I would win.

I start chiding Mila for not dropping the seduction act already. She does not react well to that. I don't know exactly what's wrong with me. I understand what she's doing. Mila is extremely strategic. She's waiting for exactly the right time to drop Silvey's ass and claim his throne. And it's not as if she's dropped me. She still shows up at my place late at night, still wants me to hold her after she escapes from his greasy hands, still likes to daydream with me about what life on Kepler will be like when we finally get there. Sex is off the table until she doesn't have to associate it with Silvey, but kissing is fair game. I make sure that Mila is always in control with me. She has to be. The goddess *needs* to know I'm nothing like Silvey.

But it still grates on my nerves to watch what Silvey's doing to her.

"I thought she was *your* girl?" Zaden says to me after a particularly horrendous display of public ownership occurs during a ship status update broadcast. Silvey pats Mila's butt on-screen before asking her to take over the update for him. Her face is nothing short of mutinous.

I'm irritated by the question. "Mila isn't anyone's girl," I snap. "It's up to her to decide what she wants to do with that asshole."

"I don't know how you can be okay with her sleeping with that guy, though," Phelps says. "She deserves a whole hell of a lot better than that creep."

This coming from a guy who was known on Earth for bringing home girls forty years younger than him. And Phelps hasn't gotten better on this ship. There's something about a trip like this that encourages bad behavior. I've noticed that the farther we get away from Earth, the looser everyone's morals become. Phelps isn't the only one sleeping with anyone on board who will tolerate him for more than fifteen minutes. We better hope the Immortality Virus really does make us mostly immune to STDs, or everyone's going to have herpes within the next year.

Our bad behavior is by no means limited to especially salacious behavior, either. Petty theft has become a thing on the ship. There's a rumor that at least one gang has formed, though none of my friends have been invited to join, and violent fights are breaking out. Some guy died in a brawl last week, and Mila had to create a whole penal department to deal with the issue. Guess we're all going stir crazy faster than expected. I blame my own jealous ape feelings on whatever's making everyone else feel like social etiquette is no longer a high priority.

But I don't want to be this way with Mila. It's not me. I'm the type who gets rid of someone who hurts Mila, not the type who boils under the collar while she lets herself get hurt by another man. I focus on wanting to snap Silvey's neck whenever I see him and try not to transfer any of my irritation to Mila. My efforts are futile. We end up having a nasty argument about it anyway.

It happens one evening after I see him kiss her in public. In front of his wife, who smiles at them like it's both consensual and cute. As if she and Mila are just Silvey's little pets and everyone needs to get over it. I see red when it happens, and I *know* if I got into it with Silvey right then, I *would* kill him. But instead of initiating that, I storm to Mila's private cabin and wait there to confront her about it.

As soon as she returns, I lay into her. Hard.

"Why don't you just tell him to back off?" I demand. "You don't need him for anything anymore. He needs you for everything. You're the one with all the power."

She looks at me like she's not sure she recognizes me, and to be honest, I don't recognize myself. I've never been so forceful about telling her what to do. But this isn't right, and I'm sick of it, and I really don't care if I'm pissing her off.

"He's still the captain, Christian," she says. "He could still punish me for anything he got it into his mind to punish me for."

"No, he couldn't," I say. "People on this ship are loyal to *you* now. Haven't you noticed? I hear Delphine Vardelle talk about you like you're some kind of superhero genius. Eldrye Dresden always backs her up. People know you saved the hydroponics farm and you kept us from going off-course after that last debris shower. They know you're the one who's going to get this ship safely to Kepler. Silvey needs you. You do not need him."

"Well, I'm *sorry*, but I disagree. *You* may not have to fear for your life around him, but *I* do."

Her face is flushed, and it's kind of a turn-on to see her angry. I never thought it would be. It shouldn't be. But it is. Which makes me angrier.

"He's not going to kill you for telling him to get his grimy hands off you."

"He could."

"Then *maybe* you should kill him first."

She glares at me. "Maybe *you* should tell your friend Zaden to stop hanging out with Wren. Do you know they're tight these days?"

I am surprised by that, and outraged. "What? Z? Hanging

out with that stupid woman who thinks she's God's gift to science when really, she's just God's greatest fraud?"

"The one and the same," Mila says smartly. "Zaden is sleeping with her. Did you not know? I learned after someone told me *you* were sleeping with her."

I wouldn't touch Wren with a ten-foot pole, and Mila knows it.

"Well, at least he's not screwing the captain," I mutter. It is a mistake. I know it is. I shouldn't have said that. But I only feel angrier when she calls me on it.

"What has gotten *into* you? Are you *jealous*?"

"I don't know. What has gotten into *you*? What are *you* so *afraid* of?"

We find ourselves in a glare-off that lasts until the rage on her face seems to quell for a moment. It's the calm before the storm. We're still standing outside the door to her cabin, but she was at least an arm's length away from me before. Now she steps forward until her face is mere inches from mine. I fight a tremble.

"You know, I thought you were different from Silvey," she says viciously, "but maybe all men are exactly the same."

"I *am* different," I whisper.

Her eyes flash their brightest red at me. "No." She points her finger sharply into my chest. Her fingernails gouge my skin through my shirt. "You're just like all the other men out there. You *want* me to feel vulnerable."

That takes my breath away. "I have *never*—"

"And I *hate* feeling vulnerable. I hated feeling that way when I didn't think I would ever get on this ship. I hated feeling that way when that slobbering man assaulted me. I hated feeling that way watching my brother die. I hate feeling that way whenever Silvey makes me do *any*thing, and I hate feeling that way with *you*, Christian Godric."

The last thing I ever wanted was to make Mila Hildebrand feel vulnerable. I am cut deep by her words. I don't even see where she's coming from.

"But I don't ever make you do—"

She laughs loudly and wickedly. "Oh, you don't think you're doing anything wrong? You think you never make me do anything? But you play this game with me where if I want something from you, I have to ask you for it. *And be precise Mila. Because I wouldn't want to make you do something you don't want to do.*"

I am terrified of this Mila, but I *am* like Silvey in at least one critical way I cannot deny. I need her, not the other way around. Also, maybe it's twisted on my part, but I want to kiss her.

"That is not me trying to make you vulnerable," I attempt to explain. "I'm trying to make sure you always have control. I don't want you to feel—"

"Bullshit." Her face is screwed up into a scowl. "You've been telling me since I met you how powerful you think I am. Well, if I'm so powerful, why do you think it would be so *easy* to make me do something I don't want to do? Who do you think you are? Some narcissistic, manipulative, egotistical god?"

I can't look away as she holds my gaze straight on, and maybe she has a point here, too. I *am* narcissistic, manipulative, and egotistical. I have thought of myself as a god among humans. But I've only ever thought of myself as a minor god compared to her. I've always expected her to be more powerful than me. All I've ever wanted is to see her recognize that power. To be strong enough to demand control in whatever way she wants it.

Are we finally there? There seems to be a fire raging out of control in her eyes, but she's standing her ground.

"Has it ever occurred to you that maybe I could handle it if you wanted something from me that I wanted to say no to? Or that maybe I'd *like* for you to have some preferences? That I'd *like* to feel desired by you? I'd *like* to hear you say 'I love you' without me having to say it first?" She curls her hand into a fist and screws it up against my chest. "Why do *I* always have to make the first move, Christian? Why am *I* always the one doing the work? Do you know how *weak* that makes me feel?"

I am now both trembling and salivating. Like a wolf amped up on adrenaline. I want to lick all the wounds she's exposing clean, and at the same time, I want to pounce all over her. I have never wanted that before. Before, it would have felt like a power play. So maybe I didn't think she had the confidence to take that before. Things have changed.

My answer comes out sounding raspy and low. "Exactly what *work* do you want me to be doing for you, Mila?"

She is utterly enraged by that. She pounds my chest with that fist. "No!" she shouts. "We're not doing *this*. I'm not telling you *exactly* what I want. Not this time. This time, *you* figure it out. You tell me what you want. You try to get it. And I'll allow it if I want it!"

She crosses her arms petulantly and for what feels like a full five minutes, I keep my eyes locked on hers while I work up the nerve to do what I've held back from doing for years.

Finally, I weave my fingers through her hair, allowing the ire in her eyes to spur me on, and I say, slowly, "I love you. I have always thought you were more powerful than me. And you have … the sexiest pout." Then I kiss her. Without asking first. Without waiting for anything. Without a sign that she's where I am. I kiss her without knowing if she'll kiss back. But she does. She kisses back hard, and it's the kind of thing that makes everything seem like such a frenzied rush for the next several minutes that it doesn't even occur to me that we're still standing out in the hall until she eventually says, "In my cabin, *now*."

Once we're inside, things intensify, and this is much better than anything we've ever done before, because she's still thirsty, but for the first time, I let her feel that I am too, and the equality of it makes this a blissed-out euphoria. Time is non-existent for the duration. I have no idea how long it's been—a few minutes? A few hours? A few lifetimes?—when I find myself hovering over her, with all the layers stripped away. I've left bite marks on her shoulder, and there are scratches on my chest that might be bleeding. I tilt her neck and fight for breath control while I murmur into her ear, "I know ... you aren't ... mine. But ... I *do* want you, Mila. Can we ...?"

She laughs, and it is exactly the way I always imagined she'd laugh if she could ever get off on the power trip she needed to feel truly in *charge*. But she doesn't say yes. She pushes me off her, and she looks utterly wanton, and I am beyond frustrated, and yet, I have the feeling that this is the start of something amazing.

She leans away from me, completely nude and totally unashamed, and looking every bit like a true goddess. "I *don't* belong to anyone," she tells me. "I never will. Not even you, Christian." She smiles. "But I'm going to end things with Silvey. Because I want you, too, and I don't want that tainted with *him*."

I shut my eyes briefly for a moment of calm, then I open them again and clear my throat. "Let me know if there is anything I can do to help you with that. I'd rather not wait another decade."

She laughs again. That wicked laugh is my new favorite thing, and it is the best thing I have ever heard.

10.

MILA

I have spent years dreaming about life on Kepler, but what I want to do for the next few weeks is just spend all my time with Christian Godric—ideally in his cabin instead of mine because his is cushier. I don't know what came over me the night he confronted me about Silvey—I don't know what came over *him* that he felt he had the right to confront me— but I know what happened was exactly the fight we needed and exactly the outcome we wanted.

I've never felt so *even* with him before. I thought before that maybe I entertained him. That maybe he liked manipulating me. I was never *sure* that he loved me. He would say he wanted me to be in control, but I don't think either of us knew quite what that was supposed to mean. Before last night, we didn't know how satisfying it would be for both of us if I had plenty of opportunities to say "no" *or* "yes."

We know now. And I know that things with Silvey are over once and for all. I will never allow that oaf to put his hands on me again. I'm not sure I'll ever let *anyone* but Christian touch me again. I can't even compare how I feel when I'm with Christian to how I feel when I'm with Silvey. Being with Christian is a form of art. It does make me feel powerful, but also beautiful and alive. Being with Silvey is a form of self-disrespect. It only ever makes me feel weak, ugly, and numb.

I wake up with a heightened sense of awareness about what I have to do now. Christian was right. People on the ship know me. I don't have to go to any of the cafeterias for breakfast. I go straight to my office, and someone has already ensured that coffee and breakfast are waiting for me there.

Also, I have allies. Many of them. Delphine and Eldrye stop by first thing to run some new ideas about Kepler by me. Christian's buddy Phelps calls me from the resource distribution center to ask what I want to do about a shortage of soap that we won't be able to remedy until we can remedy a problem with our olive production. A guy named Fergus, a civilian I recently named head of our new security team, comes by to give me our daily crime briefing.

Fergus is particularly fun for me since I found him all by myself, and he is so pleasantly respectful. He only ever calls me "Ms. Hildebrand" or "ma'am." But his brief troubles me. We've been dealing with petty theft, vandalism, and minor altercations for a while. Today, however, Fergus reports two major assaults, ten domestic abuse complaints, several break-ins, and a suicide from an overdose.

"That's a significant uptick," I say to Fergus.

"Yes, Ms. Hildebrand, ma'am," he says. "If I were on Earth, I'd say it's like we're dealing with a full moon, but we don't have any moons around here to cause this, and it only gets worse and worse."

Hmm. So Christian and I have both been on edge, and we're generally seeing behavior that is far more reckless and violent than normal all around the ship …

"Ma'am, I also received a tip that a couple is expecting," Fergus tells me.

"Expecting what?" I say.

"Baby, ma'am."

I am floored by that one. Immortals can get pregnant, but it's incredibly stupid to allow it to happen because the babies are usually mortal. Also, the ship can handle losing passengers, but our resources are very carefully controlled. We cannot have an influx of babies, and the passengers know it.

"What do you want me to do about it, ma'am?" Fergus asks.

I feel cold saying this, but I have to look out for everyone and there are policies. Social contracts we all agreed to in writing before we got on this ship. "Arrest the pregnant woman. We'll have to terminate it. And don't keep it a secret. People need to know this is unacceptable so it doesn't happen again."

Fergus nods. "Yes, ma'am."

He goes away, and I'm left with a stack of other issues to deal with before my next meeting in an hour. The nav team needs to speak with me, then I'm getting an engineering update. I have no idea what Silvey does all day long anymore because Christian was right about this, too. No one brings problems to Silvey anymore. They come straight to me, they listen to what I tell them to do.

They trust me. Not Silvey.

So that afternoon, when Silvey stops by my office like he has so many times in the past to be "briefed" about what's going on, I tell him I'm too busy to see him.

"I'm sorry?" he says. "You're what?"

"Silvey, I have a ship to oversee," I say crisply. "I don't

have time to waste with you today."

He looks wounded, and I feel the slightest twinge of sympathy for the man who valued my body enough to get me on this ship and was willing to use my mind enough to walk me right into this office.

"Can we have dinner later?" he asks. Like a little boy who's been cut off from his favorite toy. But when he moves in closer and tries to reach for my waist, I'm reminded why I don't feel like indulging him anymore.

"No," I tell him. "We're not going to be seeing each other outside a professional context anymore, Silvey. I'm no longer interested."

Now he moves from looking wounded to looking angry, and he starts sputtering out a string of dribble. "Oh, I see what's going on here. You think you're more important than I am all of a sudden. Well, I put you where you are now, Mila, and I can put you back where you were." He comes close again, and I realize his breath reeks of alcohol. Has the captain been day drinking?

I push him back. "I told you no, Silvey."

He grabs my wrists, starts trying to rip open my blouse, and I think about what Christian did to Bray long ago. If Silvey forces himself on me, it won't end well for him.

But Fergus randomly shows up right then, and it barely takes him a moment to restrain Silvey, who starts shouting that he's the captain, and how dare some *civilian* try to restrain him.

"Sir, from what I can tell, you're drunk and you were trying to hurt Ms. Hildebrand," Fergus says calmly. He's much larger than Silvey, and I chose Fergus because my research into his background told me he'd be the one I could trust in a situation like this.

"What do you want me to do with him, ma'am?" Fergus asks me.

Silvey looks at me like he's just realized that he's losing. I meet his gaze coldly. He has used me for years, and when I told him I was done, he thought he'd just take what I wasn't willing to give. I have half a mind to tell Fergus to gift Silvey to Christian.

But I need what happens to Silvey to be more legitimate. Silvey's ass is saved by my need to be strategic about my reputation.

"Put him in one of the prison cabins to dry out," I tell Fergus. "We'll deal with him tomorrow."

Silvey has already made my day long, but it's about to get worse. The situation with the pregnant woman turns out to be a disaster for me. The pregnant woman is Wren Augur. And just as my day is ending, Christian's old friend, Zaden, shows up at my office waving a damned gun around.

He comes in, points the gun at me, and says, "I always knew you were a bitch, manipulating Chris for all those years, but I didn't know you'd go this far."

The Eden Immortality has an impressive supply of guns, explosives, and ammo. It is for worst-case scenarios. Like if we happen to run into a fleet of aliens from another planet, and the aliens threaten us. Or if we land on Kepler and the native intelligent life isn't friendly.

Civilians were also allowed to bring guns. One each. I was not in on the decision to allow this, but I don't disagree with it. I, of all people, should know what it's like to get stuck living under an unfair leadership team.

Mutiny always needs to be a choice.

I believe this even while Zaden's hand is shaking as he points his handgun at me. Cold sweat runs down my neck. I didn't bring a gun myself, and it's not like I have bodyguards outside my office. Though *that's* going to change after this.

"Just calm down, Zaden," I say. "And tell me what you're upset about."

He cocks the gun, and I'm sure all the color has drained from my face, even though I'm trying not to look terrified.

"Call the med bay," he says. "Make them stop the procedure."

So much has happened today that by the time this occurs, it takes a second for me to figure out what the "procedure" even is. But I knew Zaden was sleeping with Wren, so I put the puzzle together fast.

"It's yours," I say. "You're the father."

Zaden is sweating profusely. "Yeah. And I'm not going to let you hurt Wren."

I sigh. "Zaden, no one is hurting Wren. We're just terminating the pregnancy. Wren's going to be fine after."

"You think it's just *fine* to force her to abort a baby? You're *deranged*." Zaden stalks closer to me, and I have obviously said the wrong thing. I have *got* to stop assuming that other people are as rational as I am.

"We do not have the resources to allow couples to have children on this ship," I tell Zaden. I don't think that argument is going to help anything, though. He clearly doesn't care that they broke a huge rule. "Everyone on this ship knew that when they boarded. There's a reason we made so many birth control options available."

Of course, we *will* need to be able to procreate once we're on Kepler. But in the meanwhile, every passenger was encouraged to undergo a reversible structural sterilization process.

It was optional, but everyone signed a social contract before they came on board. One of the terms was that any pregnancy would be terminated. It's terrible, but I'm hardly making this decision myself. This is simply what has to be done.

Zaden grits his teeth. "You are *not* going to kill my baby. Call the med bay. Get the doctors on the line. Stop the procedure. Or I'll kill you."

I hold my hands up in the air. "Okay. Fine. I'll call the doctor." I pick up a com, keeping my eyes on Zaden and that gun the whole time, and call the medical bay. A nurse answers the phone. "This is Officer Hildebrand," I say. "I need to speak to the on-call doctor."

"I'm sorry, ma'am," the nurse says. "But Doctor Blacklace is currently in a procedure."

I see Zaden's eyes flash with rage. He knows what that means. So do I.

"This is an urgent matter," I tell the nurse. "I need the doctor to stop that procedure immediately."

There is a pause on the line, and the nurse says, "I'll see what I can do." Then Zaden and I stare at each other in silence. Wren is still going to have to terminate that pregnancy. There is no choice. But we clearly have to restrain Zaden first.

The nurse comes back on the line. "I'm sorry, ma'am," the nurse says. "The doctor says they completed the abortion ten minutes ago."

Zaden's face falls a million miles, and I know I'm in trouble. He glowers at me like I'm some dictatorial ruler instead of just the woman at the helm of this ship, trying to make smart decisions to ensure a successful journey with minimal death.

"You *bitch*," he seethes. "You killed my son."

I am sure that right then, he's going to kill me, but Christian shows up exactly when I need him. He's out of breath—he must have run here—and he's carrying a gun, too. Something that looks a little scarier than what Zaden's got. Maybe a rifle? I didn't even know Christian had a rifle.

"You mean your *baby*, right, Z?" Christian says, and Zaden spins around so that now they are pointing their guns at each other.

Zaden begins to weep hysterically, and now I'm terrified that he's going to kill me *and* Christian.

"I had a son, Chris," he says. "I had a son."

"Your son died thirty years ago," Christian says. "Mila didn't have anything to do with that."

I'm not sure Zaden understands the difference, though, and he may not care. He keeps saying, "She killed my son. I was going to have a son."

"Zaden, set down the gun," Christian says firmly. "Now."

Zaden shakes his head. "She has to pay." He turns toward me and points the gun at me again. "She's *evil*, and she has to pay."

This whole interaction has taken ten minutes, maybe twelve, though it seems like a much longer time has passed. I am sure this is the end for me. Will it hurt when Zaden kills me? Will I know it happened? Will Christian be okay if I die today?

I don't have to find out. Christian steps in slowly behind Zaden, angles his rifle so that a shot won't hit me, and fires at Zaden before Zaden makes up his mind to shoot me. Zaden looks a little surprised as blood blooms from his flesh.

"But, you were supposed to be my best friend," Zaden garbles to Christian, and by the time Fergus shows up, Zaden is dead.

"I should have been here," Fergus says to me woefully. I like him. He's good and loyal.

But my eyes are locked on Christian, who seems cool and collected as he stares at Zaden's body like he's looking at a stranger. "It's okay," I tell Fergus. "Christian handled it."

"Well, I'll handle it from here, ma'am. But we should talk about building you a better security team tomorrow," Fergus says.

"Yeah," I agree. "That would be best."

"No," Christian says. "I get to be the one who throws him into space."

Fergus looks at me, and I nod, and we all go together to the nearest airlock, where some of our astronauts assist Christian in suiting up and securing himself to the ship. They don't even question why we need to dump a body. They open the airlock from our side, and Christian carries Zaden's body into the chamber. They shut our side, Christian presses a button to open the airlock, and I watch through a window as he tosses his friend into outer space.

Fergus whistles low next to me while it's happening. "Damn," he says. "Guess I can see why you picked him, Ms. Hildebrand, ma'am."

Once that deed is over, I take Christian's arm, and we walk together to his cabin. He puts the gun away, and gets out a bottle of whiskey, and we have a short and useful conversation about the situation while he's pouring us both drinks.

I say, "How did you know I needed you?"

He says, "Phelps called and told me what was going on. He thought Zaden was unhinged, and he was worried about you."

"What kind of gun was that?" I ask.

"Assault rifle."

I nod. "I had Fergus put Silvey in a jail cabin today. For getting aggressive with me after I told him no. Are you going to kill him, too?"

Christian sips his whiskey. "Yes. But not until killing him would help you. We can decide together when it's right. Are you okay with that?"

I sip my whiskey, too. It burns my throat in just the right way, and I am appreciative of Christian's sense of consent. "Yes. That would be fine with me."

We look at each other, and I feel the same tiny smile creeping up on my face that I see sliding over his. "So, that's the end of me and Silvey," I say.

Christian downs the rest of his whiskey and sets the glass down with a satisfying clunk. Then I barely have the chance to get in another sip of my own whiskey before he's drinking me up. It's a continuation from last night, except this time, I never say "no."

Somewhere after midnight, with his arms wrapped around me, his head resting in my lap, and my fingers stroking his hair, he says, "I'm going to make it my job to worship you forever."

I laugh. "Immortality doesn't give us forever. One day, we're going to die."

He looks up at me. "We should clone ourselves, so that if we ever get old enough that our organs are failing or we ever have major injuries or something, we always have extra parts available."

"To what, *harvest?* That's horrible." I think of the logistics and imagine slaughtering someone who looks identical to me for the sake of cutting out her liver or her left arm or something.

"No, it's not," he says. "We'll make clones and raise a set every hundred years or so. Every time we make a Christian clone, we'll make a Mila clone. So they'll always have someone who understands everything about them. And they'll pretty much live above the law like we will, and they'll have everything they ever want, and we'll only use them for parts if we absolutely have to."

I yawn. "Sounds dangerous. What if one clone set outsmarts us and tries to overrule us?"

Christian sighs like he is extremely satisfied. "Then, we absolutely deserved it."

11.

CHRISTIAN

A month goes by. Two months. Four months. A year. Mila keeps Silvey locked away that entire time, and no one—not even his wife—misses him while she takes over completely. Mila is overwhelmingly popular with both the crew and the civilian passengers.

Though one of her first goals is to tear down the divide between crew and civilian.

"We're creating a new civilization here," she tells us. "Every person on this ship needs to function like a part of a well-oiled machine. Everyone in their place. Everyone doing what they're best at. No one wasted. There should be no difference between crew members and civilians."

She is good at reading people, so she is good at putting people to their best uses. I think maybe this is because she's such a nerdy introvert at heart. She spent years watching the people around her, learning their weaknesses, their strengths. I listen to what they say about her now. They call her inspiring. Say that she truly respects her people. That she's a great leader. That she's a genius.

"You know the thing I'm most afraid of?" Phelps says to me one day.

"Going off the deep end like Z?" I say. Because that's what I'd be most afraid of if I were Phelps. He must know now I'd kill him to protect Mila if I had to.

"Nah, that would suck, but everyone dies sooner or later." Phelps smacks my back. "And you're not cruel to people who are loyal to you. I trust that you'd kill me fast if I tried to hurt the Empress."

That's what they've started calling her. Behind her back. I may or may not have started it.

"So, what then?" I ask.

"I'm afraid of disappointing her." Phelps stares off into the distance while he says this. "She says I'm the best person on this ship when it comes to resource logistics. As long as I'm constantly monitoring things, there's never a time when we're blindsided by a shortage of anything. And she trusts my team to come up with solutions when we do have shortages." He shakes his head. "I don't know, man. I just, I want to live up to that, you know?"

I doubt I'll ever have to kill Phelps.

Though you never know. It's a damn good thing that Mila is so good at appealing to people whose egos need to be stroked and inspiring the ones who don't need that, because as time goes by, we're all becoming unhinged. Mila has to keep everyone busy, or this place would be a zoo of rabid monkeys. Fornicating in public is now strictly forbidden because, as Mila says, "gross." Stealing someone's sweater can earn you a month in an isolation cabin. Get drunk and punch the guy sitting next to you for fun, and you might find yourself restricted from alcohol for the next century.

It's not happening to everyone exactly the same, but it's

happening to all of us. Mila's patience is thinner every day, and she's acquiring what seems like almost a taste for being ruthless when necessary. I think she likes it when she has to order her top guard, Fergus, to take down someone who's being difficult. Good thing Fergus seems to get off on both the power trip and the puppy dog worship he has for Mila. He is so excessively loyal that I may have to kill him one day, just to prevent him from trying to topple me. After all, I like to think I am Mila's last line of defense, and I always will be.

But she keeps me happy with Fergus by allowing me to handle what she calls the "difficult" cases. The times when we need information from someone. Or when we need to persuade them to do something they don't want to do.

"It's just that you're so good at torture and manipulation, Christian," Mila tells me whenever I have moments of doubt. Usually, these conversations occur in private, at my place. She's taken over Silvey's cabin as her own, and we make use of both locations, depending on her mood. I still think of what Mila and I do together in private as the perfect balance of pain-pleasure, but she is correct that my place is more frequently utilized for the pain end of the spectrum.

I wonder, did I have violent tendencies from the beginning? Perhaps. Violence is such a fascinating form of passion. But the longer I live, the easier it is to snuff someone out when the universe would be better off without them, and the more I enjoy dragging it out. Which is to say, anyone who really seriously threatens Mila ends up on my turf. Even Fergus likes turning the truly despicable ones over to me. He calls me "The Vigilante," but I am not a good guy, and I'm earning a reputation myself. People know I'm Mila's top adviser. They know she only ever sleeps with me. They know what happens when someone crosses me.

They don't cross me.

About two years after Silvey is ousted, the Eden Immortality gets a communication from Earth, and Mila calls all her top advisers in for a meeting.

I, of course, know about what's happening before anyone else, and I know what's going to happen now. Nothing. The communication changes nothing. But this is a test of Mila's power.

She is wearing her now-trademark heels and a black dress with sharp cap sleeves that seem to be reaching toward the ceiling of the room. She has Guasparre on call all the time. She says he's good at making her look intimidating.

She stands up to start the meeting and says, "Earth just called." Then she pauses to look around at the group she's gathered. There's brutish Fergus (security), crafty Delphine Vardelle (planetary optimization), and resourceful Phelps (resource management), all of whom I mostly like and trust. There are a few folks I'm still neutral on—Eldyre Dresden (civil accounting), Jennica Wax (navigation), Gage Melendez (astrophysics), Ramsey Nevers (engineering), and Cosimo Wheeler (passenger well-being, AKA human resources). Then there's Doctor Andrew Blacklace, who I'm suspicious of based on nothing more than a feeling that the guy always has his own agenda.

But for now, everyone is paying attention to Mila, so I do as well.

"As it turns out, the Immortality Virus is flawed. It may make us live forever, but it is also damaging our brains. The longer we live, the more the area of our brain that controls long-term, executive functioning is impaired. We are losing our ability to empathize. Our need to fulfill short-term desires is increasing."

"That explains a lot," Fergus says.

"No shit," Blacklace says. "Do they think it's reversible?"

Mila cocks her head. "Of course. They have assured me that if we turn around right now and go back home to Earth, they'll start working to correct the problem as soon as we arrive."

Dresden snorts. "They have no idea how to fix this, do they? We go home, and they turn us into lab rats for the rest of our immortal lives."

Mila says nothing.

"Well, we're not doing it, are we?" Delphine says. "If we go back, we'll never get to Kepler."

That is one reason why Mila likes Delphine. The two women agree wholeheartedly that getting to Kepler is the priority here.

"We have plenty of scientists on board," Gage says. "Is there any reason we can't attempt to develop a cure or some way to mitigate this ourselves?"

Blacklace scoffs. "We have maybe three medical researchers on this ship. That's not nearly enough to develop a cure for something like that."

Mila turns her attention to Blacklace, who has an uncanny tendency to meet her eyes straight-on without ever betraying his emotions. "Doctor Blacklace, does that mean you are in favor of returning to Earth?"

Blacklace snorts. "Fuck no. I'm not going back to be locked up in some biosphere for crazy immortals. I say full speed ahead."

"Is it really going to be that bad?" Cosimo asks. "Does this deficiency in the virus mean that by the time we get to

Kepler, we'll all be monsters or something?"

Mila stays neutral-faced. "That's what Earth is afraid of. That with this problem, we are a danger to the planet we are destined for. That when we get there, we will be hellbound on destroying it. We will show up with every intention of conquering, colonizing, and subduing Kepler unless it accepts us as its newest citizens."

"That's just ridiculous," Delphine says. "That was *always* how it was going to be. Even before we found out about this. It would be naïve to think that humanity could expand to other planets without ever threatening those planets. Exploration and expansion mean putting more than a few other species at risk."

"But failure to explore and expand means putting humanity at risk," Blacklace says. "Screw Earth. So we're not going to be as nice as they want us to be when we arrive on Kepler, is that right? So what? We can handle our own."

Mila seems satisfied with that, but she likes it when I chime in.

"We can do more than that, Blacklace," I say. "We can arrive as an organized, intelligent society of immortals with goals to build on and improve the planet."

"Yes," Mila says. "We will arrive on Kepler as far more than a group of rabid humans. We will arrive as a civilization. A nation."

"An *empire*," Delphine says. "The Immortal Empire."

Mila raises an eyebrow at that. "Oh, I'm sure Emperor Silvey will love that."

The group starts snickering.

"Funny, Hildebrand," Delphine says. "Obviously, you're the Empress. And we—" she gestures around to the rest of us "—are your loyal lords and ladies."

Mila catches my eye briefly—she suspects that somehow, this little change in titles was my doing—but she is not displeased with it. I can tell. Still, she pauses on that again, as a show of respect to everyone else in the room, and then, at last, she nods.

"Very well, Lady Vardelle," she says. "I will send a return message to Earth immediately. We are not turning back."

"Excellent, Empress," Delphine says, and Fergus cracks his knuckles, which is his way of saying, "I'm in."

"Guess I'll get to work on the cure," Blacklace says. "God have mercy on the Keplerians whose lives we disturb."

"I thought you were in, *Lord* Blacklace," I say.

"I am in, *Lord* Godric," he retorts with a hiss at the back of his throat. "But just because this is the right decision for us, doesn't mean it's going to be *good* for everyone else. Best if we all know that going in." He eyes Mila. "Don't you agree, Empress Hildebrand?"

She smiles. "Absolutely."

12.

MILA

I recall dying a lifetime ago. It was a slow, painful, exhausting, miserable march to what would have been a tragic end for a girl who was far too smart and beautiful to die so young.

There was a way to save me, but at first, no one thought I was worth saving. I didn't look like someone who had any promise as anything other than, perhaps, a pretty face. And there are plenty of pretty faces in the world. I was counted out.

Then, a stranger gave me a second chance. I don't know why. I never met her again. I never knew what made her speak up for me. But I was given an eternity to learn how to use the tools at my disposal better. It didn't come easy for me, and it wasn't without sacrifice, but I learned. I learned that life is not fair to anyone. That no one who tries to own you can truly respect you. That nothing worthwhile comes free. And that everything that matters is up for grabs if you only reach for it.

Now, at last, I am staring down at a blue, white, and green marble. It is not Earth. No, this marble is far more beautiful than Earth. Kepler is not polluted with millennia of human scum and waste. It is not paved over or blown to bits. It is a treasure trove of lush land, just waiting for the right person to know what to do with it. And under my rule, Kepler is going to be the most beautiful planet in the entire universe.

There is only one problem. Some measly mortals who raced my ship here and landed a few hundred years ago. They've had just enough time to build up a handful of fledgling nations. But they are weak and far less capable than my empire, and they will bow to me.

A man is standing next to me. He is tall and gothic pale. His eyes burn with red fire, but there is still a ring of coal behind that red.

He takes my hand and kisses the back of it. "Empress," he says. "Your planet awaits."

Lord Godric. My favorite of the lords and ladies who serve me. He is the only person who believes in me more than I believe in myself, and there is no one else I love. Our relationship is not traditional. He does not have a key to my cabin. He does not keep his things at my place. Never once has he suggested marriage. The very thought is repulsive to both of us.

After all, how can I pledge myself to one person when I am so much greater than that? I am no longer that dying girl, being counted out, relying on a pitying stranger to beg for a second chance for me. No. I am Mila Hildebrand, Empress of the Immortal Empire, and no one will *ever* count me out again. I am forever not yours. And I have eternity to make you worship me.

EPILOGUE
STELLA

6606 CE Earth

"Are you sure you want to do this?" I ask my daughter. She is stubborn. Far more stubborn than I. A quality she inherited from her father.

Hope's sky-blue eyes are steady and strong as she smiles back at me. Her hands are in mine, and she squeezes them while Alex keeps his hand on my shoulder. Alex is my solid-as-a-rock son. Always there for me. Always keeping us steady while Hope works tirelessly to fling our hearts into the galaxy.

She's already said her goodbyes to everyone else, but Alex, her twin brother, and I, her mother, love her more than everyone else. We need a long goodbye. We have more at stake if something happens during her journey. We have more to lose.

"Will it be worth it to you even if you don't find him?" Alex says. "Even if he's dead?"

Hope rolls her eyes. "He's not dead. You read the message Max Kozlov sent back. He's alive. We only need to go get him and bring him home."

"Fifty years is a long time," Alex says. "A lot can happen in a few years."

Like Hope's ship could crash or she could be abducted or she could get lost in the huge expanse of the universe on her way to a planet billions of miles away. Or something could happen to *him* before she reaches him. Though I can hardly bring myself to think like that. I never could.

Hope punches Alex's shoulder lightly. "For an immortal? Fifty years is nothing, Alex, you know that. Dad's survived thousands of years away from home, and all that time, he didn't even know we were alive. He can make it fifty more."

"And fifty back," I remind her. "You have to come home."

Hope has my smile, except that she always smiles with her teeth. She throws her arms around me. "Mom, I promise, nothing is going to happen. The warp technology is sound. The cryogenics chambers are safe. I'm going to get out there to the warp zone, slip into a nice cold bed of ice, and when I wake up, I'll be nearly to Kepler. Easy as a cinch."

I wring my hands. She's so sure she can do this. So sure she can bring her father back home. And I want that so bad, but it would be so much worse to lose her, too.

"Life is about taking chances, Mom," she says. "Isn't that what you always taught us? Sometimes, you have to take a chance on someone you love. I love you so much, but we've had thousands of years together. I want to meet my dad. I want Alex to meet him." She kisses my cheek, where a tear is sliding down. "It's going to be okay. We deserve this. *You* deserve this."

Alex slips his arms around both of us. "You've got this, Hope," he says with that calm voice that never fails to remind me of Myles. "Bring Dad home."

There are several hugs after that, and many "I love yous," and I am never going to understand what I did to deserve the blessing of these children. They were my second chance after I lost Myles. The reason I never gave up perfecting a form of the virus I could take. The reason I never stopped looking to the sky and hoping that maybe one day, I'd see Myles again.

Did you know that some people fall in love forever? It's true. There's a gene for it, and I have it, and so did Myles, and so do our children. Hope hasn't met the love of her life—she says fate will bring that person around whenever he or she is supposed to come around. Alex met the love of his life hundreds of years ago. And I met the love of mine four-thousand, one-hundred, ninety-two years ago.

I watch the launch with Alex standing right next to me, and his wife right next to him, and their three kids, and my eleven grandchildren. I get the numbers wrong after that. There are great-grandchildren and great-great-grandchildren, and they all hang onto the Kayes name, which has belonged to great senators and two presidents, several ministers, and far too many business tycoons. We have a crazy amount of security because everyone wants in on our reunions, and somehow, I'm the matron of the family, though I have never been a Kayes myself. The entire family couldn't actually fit in this room, so it's a good thing so many of them had to join us virtually.

I hold a delicate, rose gold petal, hanging on a chain Myles Alexander Kayes gave me long ago, and I watch the sky while Myles's daughter shoots into space, on exactly the kind of mission I think Myles would have loved.

And I send the same thoughts out into the universe to the man I have always loved. Be safe, and come home to me.

Because I'm yours forever, and I believe with all of me that there is no force greater than a love that makes you give your whole heart to someone else.

"A hundred years, Mom," Alex whispers to me. "We only have to wait a hundred more years."

"I can wait a hundred years," I say. "I could have waited for all of eternity."

He kisses my temple. "It's okay. Hope's going to make sure you don't have to."

The End. For Now.

But you can meet back up with your favorite immortals in:

SANDRA L. VASHER'S

SISTERS
OF THE
PERILOUS HEART

MORTAL HERITANCE BOOK ONE

Carina and Miguela turned around. A woman with enormous shoulders and scraggly hair was leering at them. She was wearing a heavyweight, multi-pocketed jacket, and a jagged knife was strapped to her arm.

"You two here for the shuttle?"

Carina took a deep breath, then wished she hadn't. The woman smelled like dead fish. "Yes, please," she said, trying not to gag.

The woman put her fists on her hips and made a "humph" noise. "It's sixty dollars a person," she announced.

Miguela, who had covered her nose, dropped her hand. "Sixty?!"

The woman leaned ominously over Miguela. "You got a problem?"

Carina counted the money out of the purse and handed it over. "Nope."

The woman stuffed their money into her jacket and pointed to Hiller's Quick Stop. "I'm Mrs. Hiller. Toilet's in the back. Twenty-five cents a flush. Next stop's six hours away."

Miguela opened her mouth, but Carina pushed her toward the shop. "You never talked back to Sister Agda!" she hissed when they were inside. Miguela stomped through the store in front of Carina. The place wasn't well stocked, and the toilet looked like no one had paid for a flush in a while. Miguela came out of the bathroom with a green face. "I had respect for Sister Agda," she said, "And I hate you."

The 'seats' were two benches facing each other in the back of the van, and four passengers were already seated. A boy with glasses was near the front, clutching a small green backpack and staring warily at the guy across from him, who was asleep and had his legs stretched out so far the younger boy was forced to tuck in his feet. The guy looked like he might be in his twenties, and he was wearing black jeans, a crisp black shirt, and a black vest.

Max was already in the van, sitting on the same side as Vest Guy, and a teenage girl was sitting between them. She had shiny, caramel-colored hair that fell over her shoulders like she never had to do anything to tame it and a cute, curvy shape. Max was chatting with her, and he didn't even make eye contact with Carina as she and Miguela got in the van. Carina's stomach churned with jealousy as she sat next to Glasses Boy, whose eyes traveled nervously toward her.

The teenage girl looked curiously at Carina and Miguela. "Poor things. Who sent you out in handmade dresses? You look like orphaned urchins."

Carina blushed, while Miguela stiffened.

"What are your names? We're going to be together for two days; we might as well be friends." She put her fingers delicately toward herself. "I'm Reed."

Carina thought Reed's voice made her sound like a high-pitched goat. Vest Guy shifted. Miguela leaned back and shut her eyes like she'd rather sleep than make friends with Reed. Max finally made eye contact with Carina. "I'm Max. Who are you, stranger?"

Reed giggled obnoxiously and put her hand on Max's knee. "You are so funny!"

Carina thought maybe she'd rather sleep than make friends with Reed, too.

Mrs. Hiller appeared at the back of the van. "These roads aren't safe. There are Red-Eyed bounty hunters crawlin' all over. I drive fast. If you get carsick, throw up in your own bag. If you have to go, hold it. We don't have heat. The windows don't open."

"Brilliant," Vest Guy said without opening his eyes.

Mrs. Hiller slammed the doors shut.

Reed inched closer to Max. "I hope it's a fast two days."

Carina hoped so too, but hours later the back of the van was freezing and dark, and Reed was still talking. Carina couldn't decide if she was more motion sick or sick of Reed, nor could she see how far Reed had scooted into Max's personal space.

And Reed was telekinetic.

She hadn't stopped talking about it for at least an hour of the miserable ride.

"I can only lift little things, like spoons and bottles and stuff, but my mom says we can't take any chances. That's why I'm going to Shadow of the Mountains. To stay with my grandma for a while. There's been even more bounty hunters in Clemson lately. And you never know who they'll turn you over to. They say Hildebrand just kills Mortals with magic—"

Max interrupted. "*Hildebrand?*"

"Yep. Empress Hildebrand," Reed said. "But she's only controlling one faction of the Immortal Empire. There's a whole faction of Immortals under Lord Godric, and he's *experimenting* with the Mortals *he* captures. Some people think he's trying to create a superior race."

Vest Guy muttered something that sounded like "vapid witch."

"If you have something to say, say it out loud," Reed snapped.

Carina felt a thrill as Vest Guy sat up.

"Fine," he said. "You're a brainless twit. If you have any telekinetic powers at all—which I doubt—you should know better than to brag to everyone about them. Any one of us could be working for a bounty hunter. As for Godric: the Immortals are already superior. Godric isn't experimenting because he has an inferiority complex. He's doing it because he's bored."

Reed tutted snootily. "You don't know what you're talking about. I bet you're in this van for the same reason I am. All dressed up and taking *this* ride to Shadow of the Mountains? What are *you* hiding?"

The van veered to the right and came to a stop. The lights in the back blinked on, and Glasses Boy gasped. Carina clutched Miguela's arm. Vest Guy looked toward Reed. He smiled. He had perfectly straight teeth. And bright red eyes.

Reed shrieked.

"Now you know," he said, and he climbed over all of them, opened the door to the back of the van, and jumped out.

ACKNOWLEDGMENTS

I self-publish my books under my own independent publishing house, Mortal Ink Press, LLC. I use a number of resources as an indie publisher, including Scrivener, FlatIcon, FreePik, Adobe InDesign, Calibre, Affinity Designer, Grammarly, Shutterstock, and so on. My cover was designed by Danielle Doolittle at DoElle Designs. Danielle is great, and I highly recommend her! I write locally with the Raleigh Pubwriters and virtually with Word Stitch Write Ins. Look either of these groups up online, and you can write with me, too.

BOOKS BY SANDRA L. VASHER

The Immortal Mistakes
Stella Rose Gold for Eternity
Lizzy Dupree and the Thousand-Year Crush
Mila Hildebrand is Forever Not Yours

The Mortal Heritance
Sisters of the Perilous Heart
Kingdoms of the Frozen Dead (January 2021)

ABOUT THE AUTHOR

Sandra L. Vasher is an indie writer, recovering lawyer, dreamer, consultant, blogger, serial entrepreneur, and mommy of very spoiled dog. She enjoys long drives in fall weather, do-it-yourself projects, animated movies and cartoons, fanfiction, red wine, traveling everywhere, and baking sweet and savory treats. She can often be found trying not to hunch over her computer at her favorite coffee shops in Raleigh, North Carolina. Follow her online at sandyvasher.com.